Also by Jill Paton Walsh

HENGEST'S TALE

The Dolphin Crossing

JILL PATON WALSH

MACMILLAN
London · Melbourne · Toronto

ST MARTIN'S PRESS
New York
1967

MACMILLAN AND COMPANY LIMITED
Little Essex Street London WC2
also Bombay Calcutta Madras Melbourne

THE MACMILLAN COMPANY OF CANADA LIMITED
70 Bond Street Toronto 2

ST MARTIN'S PRESS INC
175 Fifth Avenue New York NY 10010

Library of Congress catalog card no. 67-17767

PRINTED IN GREAT BRITAIN BY
NORTHUMBERLAND PRESS LIMITED
GATESHEAD

To Kevin

My grateful thanks are due to Mr N. L. Braund, and to many of my family and friends whose memories have helped to write this book.

Chapter One

JOHN came out of the grocer's shop, and stood a moment on the corner of the street. He stopped to put the ration books in the pocket of his blazer, and to arrange the brown paper bag with three eggs in it carefully on top of his basket. While he stood there the children came streaming out of the school on the other side of the street. First came a dark-haired, scruffy looking boy in big boots, and after him trooped a whole crowd of yelling boys, among whom John recognized the local bullies.

As soon as the group turned the corner and were out of sight of the school gates, the yelling changed to a raucous sing-song chant.

"Ya, lousy Londoner! Ya, lousy Londoner!" The scruffy boy walked on, not quickening his pace, not turning his head.

"Look out!" screamed a jeering voice, "There's a bomb coming!"

"Run for a coal-hole, quick!" suggested another.

"Go and live in Scotland—no bombs there!" cried another voice.

"That's right. We don't want you here, you and your stinking lice!" chorused the rest.

The boy was walking past John now. His face was very stiff, the lips pressed close together. John put down the shopping basket, and stepped behind him, across the path of his pursuers.

"Stop that!" he ordered firmly.

1   A*

They stopped in their tracks. Then a curious shuffling movement started among them, as the front row sidled sideways, until a space was opened down the middle of the group, and the ringleader, who appeared to lead his gang from the back, stood facing John.

"Stop what?" he said, glancing round him. It was no place for a fight. Only a little way down the road was a bus queue, shoppers were passing them, and a policeman would be along in seconds if they started trouble. And any minute the teachers would finish staff-room tea, and come round the corner on their way to catch buses home.

"I mean leave him alone. He can't help being an evacuee. So shut up."

"I don't care whether he can help it," said the boy deliberately. "I don't like him. He stinks. Of slums."

John flushed. "You ought to be ashamed of yourself!" he said. "Your father, and my father, are fighting, or risking their lives to keep this a free country, and you go picking on someone for what they can't help, like any beastly Nazi!"

There was a pause. Then John turned on his heel, and found the scruffy boy still standing just behind him, watching.

"Come on," said John to him, and they walked away down the street. This might have been a dignified way of going, had John not forgotten the shopping basket, but he had gone only a few paces, when he had to turn round and run hastily back for it. There was a roar of laughter from the gang, and the rude yells began again behind their backs.

"Get on your high horse about your dad, don't you? What about your brother?"

"Ya dirty conchie! Dirty yellow conchie!" This time it was John who walked steadily with his face set like stone. But the ordeal did not last long; the gang did not follow them.

They walked along together in silence for some way. There was nothing in particular to talk about. They passed a large poster which said,

YOUR COURAGE
YOUR CHEERFULNESS
YOUR RESOLUTION
WILL BRING *US* VICTORY

but all the rude remarks this suggested were old jokes now. They passed a newsagent, and John went in to buy an evening paper; his mother liked to see the news. The paper was full of the fighting in Norway. John expected the scruffy boy to walk on, but he was waiting when John came out of the shop.

"Is he going to thank me? I do hope not," thought John uneasily. But out of the corner of his eye he just caught a glimpse of a boy slinking back into a doorway a little way down the street. The gang had not given up after all.

"I'll walk home with you," he said to the boy.

"Don't bother—they only yell. All bite and no bark like."

"Well, they don't do either while we keep together. I'll come."

The boy put on an odd, swaggering, couldn't-care-less expression. "Please yourself," he said.

They turned up a side road. There were only a few houses along it, and then it turned into a track across a field to Hunter's Farm, the other side of the railway. But they walked past all the houses, and came to the gate into the field.

"I'm all right from here. Thanks a lot mate," said the boy.

"I'm John—John Aston."

"Oh. I'm Pat Riley. Thanks for the walk."

3

"Where are you going? I didn't know there were any evacuees at Hunter's Farm."

Again an odd expression flickered across Pat's deadpan face.

"In this here field," he declared, "there's accommodation for a small herd of cows, and an evacuee family. The farmer says will the family please mind not to disturb the cows. But he can't tell his blasted cows not to frighten my mum!" There was a hard, angry sound in his voice. John looked away quickly, embarrassed at someone letting his feelings show so much. He didn't know what to say.

"Come and look, then," said Pat, sounding angrier still. "Come slumming—unless you're afraid of catching lice!" He climbed over the gate, and plodded through the mud across the field, not looking back.

Now John too felt angry. *He* hadn't said anyone was lousy, and he was already late getting home. But if he stayed there he would be trapped into silently agreeing with the accusation, so he climbed over the gate, lowering the shopping basket over in front of him, to avoid bumping the eggs, and followed Pat, his shoes squelching in the thick mud. At the far end of the field stood a derelict railway carriage. Someone had put brown paper across the broken glass in the windows, and there was a washing line strung up between a tree in the hedgerow and the carriage roof. Some steps up to the door had been made with old packing cases and orange boxes.

"Railway hotel," said Pat dryly. They crossed the field watched by the cows, clambered up the rickety steps and went in.

Inside it was dark—the brown paper let in a dim yellowish light. Some of the seats and partitions had been taken out of the near end of the carriage, making a long narrow room. There was an old table, with a primus stove on it, and a seat still in place at the far end,

4

the plush upholstery worn bald and splitting in places. Above it the luggage rack remained—piled up with an assortment of pans and boxes, and chipped enamel plates and dishes. This was not surprising as there was nowhere else to put things. Under the luggage rack was a cracked mirror, and a map of railway routes, and with them a picture of a sunny beach, and the words "Come to Ramsgate". A hook in the roof supported a large lantern, which looked as though it had belonged to a ship. A zinc bucket stood in the corner.

From somewhere down the corridor a woman's voice called, "That you, Pat? Put a kettle on, there's a dear."

Pat dipped a mug into the bucket, and ladled water from it into a tin kettle. He set it on the primus stove, and coaxed it alight with a little meths. The flames made a steady rushing noise.

"You stopping for a cuppa?" he asked.

"Thank you; but I mustn't stay long, my mother will worry."

"All the same, ain't they?" said Pat with a grin.

"What you saying?" demanded the voice from the corridor. "You brought someone home then?" A woman came in. She looked as scruffy as Pat. Her limp hair straggled round her face, and her dress was shabby. She was pregnant, and she looked both tired and ill. But she was quite cheerful.

"Well, well, well," she said. "Here's a surprise. Visitors. Fancy our Pat having a tea-party." She looked at John. "Sit down, er...."

"John," said John, "John Aston."

"Sit yourself down, dearie," said Mrs Riley. "Bread and dripping's all there is for tea, but you're welcome."

Pat took the boiling kettle off the flame.

"Half a spoonful more'll be enough, mind," Mrs Riley warned him, as he made the tea. John had sat down on the railway seat, but Mrs Riley wanted things from the

5

luggage rack to lay the table, so she climbed on a stool, and leaned over his head. She made a great clattering as she rummaged among her stacked up pans. John ducked away, trying not to notice how bulgy she was, and flinching as he expected any minute to be brained by a cascade of falling pans.

"Here!" said Pat sharply, "You oughtn't to be doing that, Mum. Get down! Make yourself useful can't you?" he added, turning to John.

John climbed on the stool Mrs Riley had just got off, and tried to reach another mug, which she said was there somewhere. He stretched to the left, the stool wobbled, he grabbed without looking, and as he recovered his balance the whole pile of pans fell crashing over onto the floor. He had seized a handle. The noise was deafening, and it seemed to go on for minutes. He stood up on his stool, feeling a worse fool than he ever remembered, and waiting for the angry rebukes of an outraged housewife. But after the second's silence it takes to draw breath there came only laughter.

Mrs Riley laughed so much she had to sit down to it, and then just when the laugh had died down to a giggle, she saw a chipped tin mug among the jumble on the floor.

"You found it, anyhow!" she cried, and began to laugh again. Then she stopped quite suddenly, said "Nothing like a good laugh to keep you cheerful," and looked tired and ill again at once.

They sat round comfortably, and drank hot black tea out of the mugs. Pat ate thick slices of bread with dripping spread over them, and lots of salt and pepper. John said "No thank you," to several offers of a slice of this stuff, and drank his tea as fast as he could without scalding his mouth. Then he stood up to go.

"Thank you very much, Mrs Riley," he said. Only then did Pat offer any explanation.

"He heard that Bill's gang shooting off their mouths at me, and he gave them what for. Shut 'em up good and proper."

"Oh yes?" said Mrs Riley. She didn't seem interested. Pat picked up the bucket and came out with John.

"I've got to take this to the tap in Hunter's yard," he said. "Tata mate."

"Bye, Pat," said John, and began the walk back to the bus stop.

Chapter Two

THE cottage seemed quite different when he got home.
It was just the same really; red carpet down the hall, the
grandfather clock with the painted face just squeezing in
under the low ceiling; a silver tray set out for letters on a
half-moon table just inside the door. But he had never
come in before without noticing how narrow and small
it was, and this time he noticed instead how orderly and
comfortable it looked.

"John? Were the buses late? Did you get everything?" his mother's voice greeted him from the kitchen.
He could tell by her voice that she had been worried
because he was late, and he could also tell that she was
not going to say anything about it.

"All here," he said, putting the shopping bag on the
table.

"Tea is ready, dear, on the trolly beside the fire." He
went into the tiny living room, took a plate, and helped
himself to scones and butter. His mother came in with
the teapot, and poured out two cups.

"John, do remember that that butter has to last a
week!" she expostulated, watching him. "You'll never
realize that the ration has been cut."

"Oh, I know, Mother," he said ruefully. His mind
flashed pictures of great slabs of butter, too thick to
spread, piled on sticky buns. "But I'd rather eat it all at
once, and then have marge on the other days. That way
at least I can have enough to taste properly one day a

week. But you," he continued, looking with distaste at the faint scrape of yellow on his mother's scone, "never enjoy it at all."

"The Ministry of Food adviser wrote to the papers to-day saying if you put it in your mouth upside down you can taste it better. Butter side against the tongue." Mrs Aston carefully turned her scone over and put it in her mouth.

"Does it work?" asked John.

"Well ... perhaps. Just a little. Did you bring an evening paper?"

"Yes, here. Daddy's still afloat."

This was the usual butter conversation, followed by the paper conversation. They said something like it to each other every day. And usually John liked it. His mother's talk reminded him of how much better it was not to be at school; how much more comfortable it was to be bored at home. But today he was miserable. A hard angry feeling had overtaken him on the way home, and it wouldn't go away. He knew his mother knew, and would worry about it, but he couldn't stop her seeing what he felt like, however hard he tried.

"*It isn't fair,*" he thought to himself, "*she has a sort of telepathy about me, but I never know what she is thinking.*"

He picked up the paper as his mother put it down. It had a military despatch about the fighting in Norway on the front page. Beside the news release an advertisement exhorted him, "WIN YOUR WAR OF NERVES WITH SANATOGEN". He took the paper over to a table under the window. The table was covered with a large map of Norway. On the map were a lot of toy soldiers and tanks and ships. Each soldier stood for a division; the English were represented by redcoated guardsmen, the allies by other sorts. Some of the most battered had been dipped in black paint, and stood for Germans. A toy tank

9

showed a tank regiment; toy ships sailed round the blue parts of the map.

John looked at the paper, and carefully moved his soldiers and ships. It didn't look too good to him. But of course, one couldn't tell; the newspaper couldn't print everything, and there was always the R.A.F.—John had no way of showing action in the air on his map.

"I'm just writing to Andrew," said his mother from her chair. "Would you like to put a few lines on the bottom?"

"No thanks, not today," said John stiffly. This too was a conversation they had often. Why did she keep on asking when she knew he wouldn't?

"You seem a little down, dear," his mother observed.

"Well there isn't much to be cheerful about," he replied gloomily, looking at his map.

"Yes, that's true, I suppose," said his mother with a sigh. She always tried to be fair. "Oh dear," she went on, "I do hope I did the right thing taking you from school. It's really so difficult to tell. But it's dreadful not having the family near you when . . ." Her voice died away. "Mr Macleod is a very good tutor," she hurried on. "I don't think your studies will suffer. Anyway, it's a horrible thought, but you'll probably have to go into the forces as soon as you're old enough for Oxford, and you won't get to University till it's all over. And you *are* a great comfort to me." She wasn't talking to him; she had said it all to him before. She was trying to convince herself.

"That's all right, Mother," he said. "I like being here."

"But you seem so bored, poor thing. I can't help wondering if I'm being selfish."

"Look, really, Mother," he said desperately, "I wish you wouldn't worry about it. You've got enough to worry about. I like being at home. I would have worried about you, too, if I'd had to stay the other side of England, when Daddy's away, and Andrew's . . . Andrew's not here either. And I don't mind not being at school!"

"You always seemed so happy there!" said Mrs Aston in a nearly convinced tone.

He faced it. "Yes, but it would be awful for me there now. You see, well, Andrew was school captain, and people admired him, and they sort of feel that the honour of the school is at stake. And they wouldn't have much sympathy for conscientious objectors, I can tell you. I'd much rather not have to hear the things they'll be saying."

Mrs Aston winced. "What will they be saying?" she demanded.

John looked at her, not wanting to answer. Poor Mother, so pretty, so good at making them all happy when there was nothing else to worry about, so happy in her beautiful big house, and so out of place in a gardener's cottage, with the troubles of the world on her mind ... why did she ask questions when the answers would hurt her so? But he always told her the truth.

"They would say he was being a coward," he answered.

She didn't flinch. "You would have to tell them that every man has a right to follow his conscience."

"Yes," he said, "but I'm glad I'm at home."

His mother licked the envelope, and stuck down the flap.

"Mother," he said, plucking up courage, "why didn't we take any evacuees?"

"Good heavens, darling," said his mother, astonished, "We weren't even asked. We gave up our nice house for the army sick-bay, and here we are crammed into this little place—we haven't any room, how *could* we take anyone?"

"There isn't any room in here, but there are all the other outbuildings," he said.

"Gracious, John, what are you talking about? None of them is fit for people to live in!"

"There's the stable," he said. "It has a water tap, and the groom's room at the end has that old range, and it's got a hay loft."

"All very comfortable for horses!" cried his mother. "But it hasn't any flooring, and it's full of old loose boxes, and nobody would dream of putting people in there. Anyway all the families they sent to this district were found room somewhere. Not that it did a lot of good; they've all gone home again now. I wonder what will happen when bombs do begin to fall on London?"

"I'll wash up these things," said John, and wheeled the trolly away. His mother put on her coat, and went to the post with her letter.

He met her at the door when she came back.

"Would you like to take a walk?" he asked. "It's a fine evening."

"We'll miss the news," she objected.

"We could listen to the nine o'clock news instead."

"We usually listen to that as well," she said, but she came with him just the same.

He took her down the track across the fields to Hunter's Farm. To get to the track they walked up the road outside their cottage a little way, past the wide gates of their real house. Mrs Aston looked wistfully up the drive. The front of the house was square, with three rows of windows arranged symmetrically, and a large door in the middle. There were pillars on either side of the door, and a fanlight over it. His mother thought it was beautiful, and so did all her friends, but John thought it was too square; all the rooms were squarish, and the sashes in the windows were square too. His mother looked right in that house, it suited the way she walked and sat, and the way she led her life, but John preferred his room in the cottage, with its sloping ceiling, and funny lumpy walls. It was more interesting.

They walked from the road along the narrow track

between fields. Beside the track was a dyke full of green water, and tall bulrushes. There were no hedges here, the dykes kept the sheep from wandering.

When they had walked for a quarter of an hour or so Hunter's Farm came into sight. The evening light was dimming gently; but there were no lights showing in the windows.

"How far are we going?" asked Mrs Aston.

"I thought we might go through to the main road, and catch a bus home."

"Tired of walking? I thought you needed the exercise." She was mystified. But she did not object, and on they went. They walked through Hunter's farmyard, meeting Mrs Cox, the farmer's wife, coming out of the barn.

"Good evening. Lovely evening for a walk," she said, sounding friendly enough, but somehow making it clear from her tone of voice that sensible busy folk like herself had no time for such pleasures.

They climbed the stile between the farmyard and the fields. As soon as they started across the fields the railway carriage came into sight. The light in the lantern shone out clearly in the dusk; then it was blacked out suddenly.

Mrs Aston looked at it with mild curiosity.

"I, er, I think since we're here, we might call on some, some, er, friends of mine. Would you mind, Mother?"

"Well! You are an odd fellow John! What are you up to? What *is* all this?"

"Just come and look, won't you?" John was in an agony of anxiety. He didn't at all know how his mother would take it, or how Mrs Riley would take it. And Pat was so prickly and easily offended. He shouldn't have come....

They walked across the soggy grass of the field, shouldered their way through a herd of sleepy cows, and mounted the pile of orange boxes. John rapped on the door.

After a second or two Pat opened it, and stood looking blankly at them. There was an uncomfortable pause. Mrs Riley's voice issued from the room inside.

"Who's there Pat? What you doing standing there? Have them in."

"Come in then," said Pat sourly.

In they went.

"Hullo, John love. Sit yourself down then," said Mrs Riley as though she had known him for years, and directing her curious stare at his mother. He felt he ought to say, "This is my mum," but somehow he couldn't manage it.

"This is Mrs Riley, Mother," he said. "Mrs Riley, may I introduce my mother?"

"What you mean, may you?" said Mrs Riley, laughing. "You have, haven't you? Very pleased, I'm sure." John's mother was no more put out than Mrs Riley. She was rapidly looking around her, grasping the situation.

"When's the baby due, Mrs Riley?" she asked. Her voice was calm and kind. John sighed with inward relief. She was going to feel as he did.

"Three weeks the doctor says. Sooner I'd say."

"And have you anywhere to go?"

"I wouldn't be here if I had, I can tell you! All me friends have taken themselves off home, and I would too if our swine of a landlord hadn't put someone else in our rooms. The old man's off in the army, and I can't find the train fare to go looking for somewhere back home. I haven't been feeling too good, and I don't feel up to it, anyway. And this is the best they could find for us down here, so here we stop, I reckon."

"Have you any running water? How do you cook? Who's going to look after you?"

John and Pat caught each other's eye, and slipped outside, leaving their mothers to talk.

They sat on the wobbly steps, and looked at the dark shapes of the cows looming about the field in the thickening night. Pat took out a rather squashed packet of cigarettes, and offered John one.

"No thanks. I don't. I, er, don't like them, actually."

"Can't say I really like them," said Pat, lighting up. "Cor, look at that!" He pointed into the night towards the town. A single small point of light was showing. It stood out so clearly in the total darkness that it seemed to have spikes round it, like the stars on Christmas cards.

"Wouldn't be a bad idea if that flipping air raid warden went after them, instead of sitting in the hedge all night waiting for that jacket of mine to slip off our window. Our old lantern wouldn't make a blooming great firework like that even if we was to open all the windows and put a mirror behind it; nasty old blighter he is. Down on us like the rest because we weren't born here."

"Does he bother you often?"

"Him and the cows, we're lucky if we ever get a peaceful night."

"The cows?"

"Yep. Now *they've* got lice, if anyone has. They gets the itch in the middle of the night, and they comes and scrapes theirselves against the side of the carriage. There's a nice scratchy bit at the back there, and they rub their backsides on that. Corse this old thing is on springs, and when they get going she rocks from side to side like she was doing eighty mile an hour on the Brighton run. Rocks me asleep, but it frightens the old girl."

"The old girl?" said John. "Do you mean your mother?"

"She ain't my mother," said Pat. "My mum ran off with someone long ago, and me dad got himself someone

15

else. Well, he tried several, but they weren't none of them much cop till he found her." He jerked his head towards the door. "She's all right. Poor thing didn't ought to have cows scaring her, not in the state she's in."

"Perhaps my mother will think of something to do about it."

"About the cows?" enquired Pat sarcastically. John flushed, but it was probably too dark for Pat to see it. He said nothing.

"What's it to you, mate?" enquired Pat.

John thought before he answered. "Well, I just feel we're all in it together ... this war I mean. I don't see why you should have more than your share to put up with."

"This afternoon when that scum were yelling at us, they were on about you, too. Something about your brother. You one of them too?"

"One what?" said John stiffly. He had gone cold inside.

"A Conchie. You heard them. Why did they say that?"

"My brother," said John carefully, "got himself registered as a conscientious objector to military service. He volunteered to work as a medical orderly, and they sent him to a hospital in Birmingham. He was a teacher before that."

"Yellow, that lot," said Pat, deliberately stubbing out his cigarette.

"This is where I say 'Every man has a right to follow his own conscience'," thought John desperately. He bit his lip and said nothing. Pat took out another cigarette, lit it and blew out his match. At last he said, "You one of them too?"

"No, no I'm not. I'm going into the navy as soon as I can."

"It'll be the army for me. That's all right then. I wouldn't take help from one of those."

16

The door behind them opened. Mrs Aston was saying goodnight. They all said goodnight, holding the door open by only a crack, so that no light escaped. It wasn't enemy bombers they were afraid of, only the air raid warden.

Then John and his mother struggled across the field to the road. They didn't say anything at all to each other all the way home. Both of them were thinking. It was a nice thing about John's mother that one didn't have to keep up a continuous chatter with her.

As soon as they got home they turned on the radio for the news. Mr. Churchill had become Prime Minister.

"Things will go better now," said Mrs Aston. "Your father thinks highly of Winston Churchill; he said he is a great man."

And as he was climbing the stairs to bed that night his mother called after him, "John, we'll go and look at the stables together tomorrow."

"Let's, Mother," he said. "Goodnight."

Chapter Three

It didn't look hopeful. It smelt of damp air and disuse. It was dark behind boarded up windows, and a green mould grew on the inside of the stone walls. It had one large room, divided into four by ramshackle wooden partitions for loose boxes, with a passage between them. At one end there was a smaller room, the old harness room, which had a stone sink and a cold tap on one side, and an oven range made of black iron on the other. John wrestled with the tap, and managed to turn it, but no water came out.

"I expect it's turned off at the mains somewhere," said his mother. They found a ladder propped against a wall, and John climbed up it through a large square opening in the ceiling, into the hay loft.

There were no chinks of light in the roof; at least it was weather proof. But it was criss-crossed with diagonal support beams for the roof timbers; there was no useful space up here.

"How long is it since this place was used, Mother?" he asked as he climbed down.

"Ages. When I was a girl your grandmother kept a mare for riding, and we had a pony to pull a little trap, but we sold them when your grandmother died. Your father talked of making it into a garage when we bought a car.... I don't think ... It won't do, I'm afraid. It's impossible."

John sat down on a wooden bench. "Well, a lot needs doing. But it has got an oven, and running water, which is more than that railway carriage has. Pat could help me clean it up."

"Well..." said Mrs Aston doubtfully. "It needs a lot more than cleaning up. Where is Mrs Riley going to sleep? At least the carriage has separate compartments."

"We could take out two of those loose boxes to make a living space, and leave the other two as sort of bedrooms. They've each got a window at the back."

"Mmm. Perhaps. The box doors look too rotten to use. And how is it going to be kept warm?"

"Oh, Mother," he said, pleadingly. He didn't know whether the objections were just warnings that it would all be hard, or whether they were leading up to stopping the idea altogether. He couldn't bear to wait and see.

"All right dear," she said, smiling at him. "Do what you can with it. If it doesn't work we can always make a fuss with the billeting officer. I'll leave it to you. Ask for anything you want; buckets and soap and so on."

She left him standing there. *"She doesn't think it will do,"* he thought. *"That's her way of saying so."* Dejectedly he swung the door of one of the loose boxes. It jammed against the floor when it had only opened an inch or two. The hinges had rusted and sagged. *"But even without doors,"* thought John defiantly, *"It would be better than where they are."* He went in search of Pat.

Pat was sitting on the steps of the carriage, smoking, and blowing rings at the indifferent cows. John waved and beckoned from the stile, and he came slowly over.

"Can you come down to my place? I want to consult you."

"Nope. Too risky. I should be at school, and I'm skipping it."

"You must be more than fourteen, Pat," said John. "Why are you still at school anyway?" Nobody stayed in the village school longer than the leaving age.

"Well, back home, the school there had a good work-

19

shop. So I asked me dad, and he agreed, it would be a good thing if I put in an extra year. They had a carpenters course. Helped get a decent job. So I put my name down for it, and I signed the bit of paper, saying I'd stay for the whole year. So I got to. Or that's what the headmaster says. But there ain't no workshop here. The woodwork teacher draws stuff on the boards, and we put it in our notebooks, that's all. A right bore. And now what with everyone else going back there's only me and Charlie left in the class. So he's bound to notice I'm not there, and I'll catch it if he sees me around."

"But he won't see you. We're not going past the school, and he'll be teaching Charlie!"

"You got a point there," said Pat, climbing the stile.

"That's our real house," said John, as they came past it. "But we live in the lodge now. Here we are." The boys turned into the gateway. John led the way across to the stable.

Pat looked around curiously. "What you done with the horses, mate?" he asked.

John laughed. "We don't keep horses," he said.

"Oh? I thought you lot always did." John flinched at the 'you lot', and the contempt that implied, and put his next point brutally.

"Well, as we don't, we have an empty stable. So I thought if we cleaned it up a bit, you might like to move in." He expected this to make Pat angry, but Pat was too busy looking round.

"Look in here, Pat," said John, showing him the harness room. "I haven't found the mains yet, but we ought to be able to get this going. And that thing had a fire in this bit, and an oven beside it."

"My Gran had one like that," said Pat. "They work all right. Nothing to go wrong, 'cept we might have to sweep the chimney."

"And I thought if we took out two of those boxes, and

20

left the other two, it would make a sitting room and two bedrooms," John went on.

Pat walked over and put his head into one of them. "Snag there," he said. "No floor." John looked too. Under the scraps of rotten straw there was only trodden down earth. The space between the boxes, and the harness room, had been floored with big stone flags, but the rest was bare.

"Cement," said Pat confidently. "But that would be a bit of a job that would."

"Well, there are two of us."

Pat considered. "What do you do all day then?"

"I'm studying for some exams. I have to go to my tutor for an hour some afternoons, but I can work on this the rest of the day, and do my prep. in the evenings. What about school?"

"I'll skip it," said Pat, taking off his jacket. "Let's find that mains tap, and get a broom. He stopped in the doorway. "If you're sure, that is."

"Sure of what?"

"About . . . all this."

"What do you think I showed it to you for?" said John.

They raided the garden tool shed, and came back laden. John went up to sweep out the loft, and Pat set about the unwanted pair of loose boxes with an axe and a saw. When John came down again, deafened with the noise Pat was making, he found one of the boxes already in ruins.

"Wood's rotten," said Pat briefly. "Makes it easy." He had sorted out the sound pieces of wood, and stacked them carefully against the wall. John went in search of a bucket, and found it was lunch time.

Mrs Aston sent him to ask Pat to eat with them, but he refused. "I'd better nip off home. The old girl is expecting me."

When John got back to the kitchen his mother was listening, motionless, to the one o'clock news. The months of waiting were over. The Germans had marched into Belgium.

"But they are neutral, mother!" said John.

"That didn't help them last time either," she said.

John went up to Mr Macleod's house that afternoon for his weekly afternoon of lessons in Latin and Greek. When he returned, with a new map of northern France and the Low Countries, bought on the way home, he heard thumps and crashes still coming from the stable. He hadn't given Pat a thought all afternoon. Mr Macleod had talked excitedly about Hitler, and what he was doing to the Jews in Germany. He had read aloud to John from a book which Hitler had written years before, a book called *Mein Kampf*, which should have warned everyone that Hitler could not be trusted. "Ah well," he had finished up, "Only one man saw where the world was going, and it's himself in the saddle now. Churchill will see us through if anybody can. But things will be worse before they're better." He had seen John's face and added cheerfully, "Aye; but I daresay the talk in Athens was much the same before the battle of Marathon. Hae ye got it well ready to read over to me?"

John translated the story of Marathon. It was a good story—the citizens of Athens withstanding alone the might of the great Persian king. It cheered up both pupil and master.

When John opened the door his mother had a kettle on the boil.

"Ah, there you are, dear," she said. "I'm just taking a cup of tea out to that poor boy out there. He's been working all afternoon."

John poured himself a cup, took a slice of bread, spread it thinly with margarine, and thickly with plum

22

jam, and went after his mother, bread in one hand, cup in the other.

Pat was showing her what he had done. The unwanted loose boxes were cleared, the remaining ones were swept out, and the tap was running. Pat could certainly work hard.

"And what do you think that there pipe is?" asked Pat, triumphantly pointing to a black pipe that ran up the wall beside the door, and then crossed the ceiling to the kitchen door, and disappeared through the top corner of it. "It's electric light! Look, here's the switch, all broken, and that knob where it crosses the ceiling must be some sort of light-fitting."

"Gracious!" said Mrs Aston, "you have done well. And wouldn't it be nice if you could make the light work. I suppose it must be wired from the cottage, since there isn't a meter here. We'll try to find the fuse."

The boys sat down to their tea, and Mrs Aston wandered off down the garden. John knew she would go to the gate into the big garden, look through it, hesitate, and then walk round her own garden feeling guilty, and minding each weed in her beloved beds. Then she would feel guiltier still because it was unpatriotic to mind so. The army were supposed to be responsible for it all now, but they didn't do much about the garden. John and his mother had crept in and pruned the roses themselves last March. And goodness knows what the inside of the house would look like. He was glad they couldn't go in.

"You look a bit down," said Pat. "Your teacher a swine, or is it all this on the news?"

"Macleod's all right. And I like classics. It's the news really."

"You get what it's all about then?"

"How it started you mean? Not really. They do the most terrible things in Germany, but we aren't fighting

23

and hard the road may be; for without victory there is no survival."

They were all quiet when he had finished. *"If only I were old enough!"* thought John.

"Well," said his mother quietly, as always knowing his unspoken thought, "The contribution you two boys are making is to get Mrs Riley comfortably housed before the baby comes. And your war effort will go better to-morrow if you get some sleep now. Off with you Pat; see you in the morning." She opened the door just a chink to let him out.

John smiled sleepily at his mother, and climbed the stairs to bed. His tired head was full of disconnected floating thoughts. "Blood, toil, tears and sweat," a voice said to him. The nasty looking position on the map drifted before his mind, and then the victory at Marathon. He imagined the mighty, innumerable Persian hordes fleeing away before the brave citizen-soldiers of Athens. Democracy defeating tyranny. He smiled at the gas mask on his bedside table as he fell asleep.

Chapter Four

WHEN John got over to the stable next morning Pat was already there. He had brought sandwiches for lunch.

"What did your mother say about it?" asked John.

"Nothing. I never told her. Make a surprise of it, like."

"Good idea. What do you think we ought to do next?"

"Well," said Pat, "I thought I might try to make these doors into beds. If I was to fix them across the loose boxes at the back, under the windows, a foot or so off the floor, they would make sort of bunks that we could put our mattresses on. I'll have to fix 'em up good and strong; I've brought a drill and a box of screws, and I can find wood for supports from that lot over there."

It all sounded very ambitious to John. "Will you need help?" he asked doubtfully.

"Not really, mate. How about you seeing about getting some cement for them floors?"

"Fine," said John. He started for the door.

"Er, about paying for it," said Pat.

"I'll see to that."

"No you won't. What you think this is—a ruddy charity? Here, I got two quid. That ought to do it, and some over."

"But it's going towards improving our place; of course we ought to pay for it."

"Well, was you all set up to pay out making improvements if you hadn't wanted to put us in here?"

"No . . . but I don't see . . ."

"Well, I do. Look, you take the money for the 'improvements' as you call it, instead of some of the rent you won't get. The old girl can't hardly make ends meet now; she'll never run to paying rent regular."

"Rent? Who asked you for rent?" said John crossly.

"Cripes. He does think he's a ruddy charity!" said Pat, starting to assemble his drill.

John felt the swift hotness of his face which he could never manage to stop, and to his rage felt his lower eyelids prickling too. "Really, Pat," he said, exaggerating the smoothness of his voice. "Do you have to be so unpleasant about it?" He turned on his heel and went out. He went to find his mother.

She was sitting in the living-room, with a writing pad on her knees, and the sewing machine ready on the table. She seemed to have found herself a lot of sewing.

"Pat wants to pay for the cement," he told her.

"Well, hadn't you better let him, dear?" she said absently.

"But they have so much less money than us, and it's for our place!"

She put down her pen. "Look, John dear, however little money people have, they usually have their pride. They like to feel they can contribute their share. How would you feel, do you think, if you were in Pat's place?"

"I hope I'd feel grateful," he said sharply.

His mother frowned. "And isn't it uncomfortable to feel grateful? Wouldn't it be kinder to let Pat pay his share? Anyway, why should he have to feel grateful? We're supposed to look after evacuees, as part of our war effort."

"But I'm *trying* to look after him!"

"Then let him do his bit too. He's going to be living on the doorstep, John. You will have to get on with him, or it will be terribly awkward for everyone. You should have thought of that before you started this scheme."

John looked at the floor. "I only thought of getting them out of that horrible field," he said miserably.

"Dear Janjan," said his mother softly. He grimaced at the hated baby name she had never quite let him grow out of. "But now you must get on well with Pat. And since, as you say, you have much more money than he has, wouldn't it be tactful to avoid waving it all under his nose?"

"So let him pay for the cement?"

"Yes. And thank him for it. And don't suggest he joins the golf club, or buys himself a hunter and rides to hounds!"

"Really Mother, what do you take me for?" said John, half indignant, half laughing. "Anyhow, he couldn't have a hunter unless he was going to share a bedroom with it! He said he would pay for the cement towards the rent," he put in as an afterthought.

"Did he really? I must say I like your friend Pat. Tell him that as his landlady I agree with him."

John gave her a rueful smile, and went to collect the embarrassing money from Pat.

Mrs Aston returned to her writing.

"... Janjan has found himself something to do. He has made friends with an evacuee boy and his stepmother, who had been billeted in a railway carriage. The woman is having a baby; really it's disgraceful they couldn't have done better for her than that. But the evacuees are very unpopular; one hears stories of them bringing lice, and wetting beds, and behaving very badly. I suppose it's only a few of them giving the rest a bad name. Anyway, Janjan's two are very decent people. The two boys are cleaning up the stable for them. I can imagine what you will think, but they aren't doing at all badly. Janjan's not a child any more. And it will do him good to make friends with Pat; show him that there are different sorts of people in the world. He told me the other day that his school friends were horrid about Andrew. Yes, I know how sore you are about him too, but you would never think he did it from cowardice. I hope you are safe and well, my dear, we miss you, and we can't help worrying...."

John was walking towards the town with Pat's money in his pocket. "A yard of cement, and two yards of sand," he muttered to himself, to fix his instructions in his mind. He sniffed the air, and decided the wind was coming from the sea. When the wind blew from the sea it smelt of salt and ozone; when it blew off the marsh it smelt of grass; the lush smell of rank growth. On impulse he turned and took the roundabout way, across the fields to the shore. He crossed three flat fields full of grazing sheep, and then the railway, and climbed up the landward slope of the sea wall. The cool brisk sea air blew upon his face, and quickened his pace.

He liked walking on the wall. The full tide was beating upon it now. The waves struck the stepped front of the wall, dashed backwards in a high curve, and fell in foaming swathes across the blue swaying surface. The spray touched lightly on his skin. And it was odd, he never got used to it, how the great sea on his left was much higher than the green land on his right. To his right he could see inland for miles. Over there, rising straight in the middle of surrounding trees was the tower of Lydd church. If he had had time to stop he could have picked out every village on the marsh by little spires and towers, diminished by distance, but all visible across the flat miles. Once Lydd church had looked grand and high, but now it was overtopped by a group of shiny grey bubbles;—the barrage balloons floating over the Army camp at Lydd, to stop low flying aircraft. Ahead of him the coast line curved gently seawards, and on the most distant visible point stood the lighthouse of Dungeness. Down there the land and the beach were all alike; acre upon acre of shingle, corrugated by the strong waves that had laid it there. The point grew with every tide, advancing slowly into the deep channel year by year, as the sea piled up more and more pebbles, until the old lighthouse was so far from the coastline that a new one had been built. John had once liked to walk there, and watch the ships coming by, incredibly close to the shore, following the deep water, but now it was too near the camp. The place was full of sentries holding him at gun point, asking for his identity card, and telling him, in case he had forgotten, that there was a war on, and he ought to keep out of the way.

John sighed. Before the war he had taken *Dolphin* up and down the bay with his father on every fine day in summer: there were no pleasure boats now. He looked at the horizon. Sometimes you could see the coast of France, but it was not clear enough today. Out there was France, and all our soldiers, and behind them the Germans, advancing.

He turned from the wall, and down the road into the town. There were empty houses along the road; people did not come down for the weekend as they did in peacetime. Nearer in the houses belonged not to weekenders, but to local people. They looked less desolate, though war had marked them too; the gardens had been dug up to make room for Anderson shelters—ugly turf covered bumps, in which one could sit out an air-raid protected from bombs by the earth of one's garden piled over one's head. Some of the householders had criss-crossed their windows with sticky tape to reduce the danger from flying splinters of broken glass. But outside the houses the flowers in the gardens blossomed unsheltered, unconcerned. And there hadn't been any bombs. Nobody had any idea what blast and bomb damage would really be like, except from the leaflets pushed through their doors, telling them what to do, and urging them to keep calm.

In the town John went to the builder's yard. Mr Baynes was sitting drinking tea in his little wooden shed of an office, with a paper propped in front of him. He listened to John's request for cement with the air of a man upon whom unreasonable demands are made hourly.

"Cement and sand. Ah," he said. "There's a war on, you know."

"Yes," said John. "I know."

"Well," said Mr. Baynes, having given John plenty of time to withdraw his demand, and seeing that he wasn't going to, "Cement's all right, as long as you want it for something important. I mean, I'm not going to sell you cement to line a fish pond, when there's people crying out for it to make floors for their shelters, now am I? There's a war . . ."

"Yes," said John, "I know. I want it to make a floor for an outhouse, so that we can house an evacuee family."

"Ah. Of course, when them Jerries start bombing, it'll be needed even more urgent, for repairs to houses."

"Yes. But there haven't been any raids round here yet, have there?"

"Well, I wouldn't say that quite. No, I wouldn't say that. There's a ruddy great crater where a bomb fell last week over at Sayer's Farm. Twenty feet deep, and twenty feet wide. Sayer says he can't find out if he's supposed to fill it in, or the War Office. 'Course, it's not a raid that causes *repairs*, I'll grant you that."

"No. So can I have some cement? It isn't rationed after all."

"Well, if you put it like that, yes you can. It may be rationed before we're much older. But yes, you can. Only a reasonable amount, mind."

"A yard, and two yards of sharp sand."

"Ah," said Mr Baynes, with an unmistakable note of

32

triumph in his voice, "You've got me there. No. Cement yes, sand no."

"Why not?"

"I had the army in here yesterday," said Mr Baynes impressively, as though he had been visited by a division at least, "Requisitioning. Nearly all me cement, and *all* me sand. For sandbags. Coastal defences they're making. Anyway they've took all me sand. Down to the last grain. And nearly all me cement come to that. You're lucky to get that." A happy smile suffused his face. "Very sorry, but there it is."

"Where might I get some do you think?"

"Don't know about that then. They were after all the sand they could get. I expect they'll have been just about everywhere."

John's face fell. "There must be somewhere I could get some."

"Well, if you don't mind a bit of heaving, you could always go and get some off the beach. Take it from just below the wall, where it's got some grit in it, and it'll be just right. And free, too."

"Why can't the army get it off the beach then?"

"They'd have to heave it, wouldn't they? They've got enough trouble shoving it into sacks, and piling them up. They've got enough to do."

"Yes. I'll do that then. Thank you. Send the cement up as soon as you can, please."

"Right away, before they come back, and nab that too. If the van works that is; someone siphoned all the petrol out of my tank yesterday, while I was out of the yard for a bit. Don't know what's the matter with some people. No patriotism, that's what."

John pretended to listen as he walked away. It was annoying about that sand. They would need a shovel and a wheelbarrow, and it would take time, and hold up the work. He went down the High Street to the ironmonger's shop, and bought a large trowel. On his way to the bus stop he passed the newsagent, and he went in to buy another paper. On the counter stood a large scrawled notice:

'Owing to the national paper shortage we cannot obtain enough copies of morning papers to supply all our customers. Those who order from us regularly come first.' Against this a smaller notice said '*Times, Express, Telegraph* sold out.'

John bought the *Mail*. He looked at it as he stood at the bus stop. Half the front page was a photograph of a road in Belgium. The road was full of refugees, walking, carrying their children, wheeling carts and barrows piled high with household goods. At the front of the picture was a woman with tears pouring down her cheeks. At the back was a tank, held up by the crowds choking the roads. The driver of the tank looked straight ahead over the heads of the throng. His face was blank. His uniform was British.

"He's facing the wrong way," thought John, worry tightening his throat. *"He's retreating. Don't be silly,"* he told himself. *"Tanks move in all directions. That's why they are so useful, they are mobile."* He folded the paper, and put it under his arm. But when he got onto the bus he found himself sitting opposite a man reading the same paper, holding it open, so that John could still see the depressing picture. The man was reading the sports page. He looked unconcerned.

It was lunch time when John got back. He brought Pat a cup of tea to drink with his sandwiches, and looked admiringly at the first bunk, which was already installed. Pat was very good at making things; John felt envious. While he was eating his rice pudding, sitting at the kitchen table, for the cottage had a large kitchen and no dining-room, Pat came to the back door to return his

34

cup. John grinned at him, and put more plum jam onto the remains of his rice.

"Er, Mrs Aston," said Pat, "I'm drinking a lot of your tea. I'd better get my mum to give me some sugar for it. Mustn't use your ration."

"That's all right, Pat. Don't worry. I expect your mum is finding it hard to make do now the ration is cut, without giving it away."

"What about you?"

"Well," said Mrs Aston, her face showing a slightly guilty expression, "As a matter of fact we've got plenty. My husband brought some from the States when he docked last time. It's for jam making really, but we've more than enough. Don't worry."

"Right. Thank you. And have you got a wheelbarrow we could borrow?"

"Whatever do you want a wheelbarrow for?"

"We have to fetch sand from the beach, Mother," said John, "I couldn't buy any this morning. It's all being used for sandbags."

"There's one in the garden shed, beside the potting shed in the big garden, if I remember rightly. I don't see why you shouldn't take that."

John finished his rice, and they went to look. They walked through the gate that led from the cottage garden into the real garden, and took the path through the shrubbery and into the kitchen garden. The kitchen garden was a great mass of weeds—sorrel and docks and nettles growing up and choking the fruit bushes.

"You mean to say all this was yours?" said Pat.

"Yes. It was nice when it was looked after well. We had lots of fresh vegetables from here."

"Daft, ain't it, sending land girls swarming everywhere to keep up farms, and letting this lot grow weeds?"

"Yes, I suppose it is. Look, over there, there's the tennis court."

They looked at it mournfully. One of the posts was sagging slightly. The white lines were faded, and a few tufts of grass had taken hold on the tarmac. Beyond the tennis court stretched the lawn running across to the house. The boys stood and looked at it. Around the lawn the rhododendrons were in blazing flower.

As they stood there an army ambulance swung round the bend in the drive, and stopped outside the door. The drivers got out and opened the back. Uniformed orderlies came out of the house to help, and they carried out four stretchers. The men on the stretchers were wounded. The right arm of one of them dangled, and they could see caked mud on the khaki sleeve. And one of them had no face; only bandages wound round and round his head. The bandages were blotched with the brown stains of dried blood.

The boys watched while all four stretchers were carried indoors, and the ambulance had driven away. They said nothing.

John felt chilled, as though the sun had suddenly gone in.

Chapter Five

"How about that barrow?" said Pat at last. They got it, and trundled it back to the stable. It was a large, solidly made wooden one, and it was heavy.

"Job for two," said Pat laconically. "And right charlies we're going to look, too, trotting along the road with this."

"Let's go across the fields instead," said John. "We could make for Crossman's boatyard, and go down the slipway onto the beach. It would be a lot easier than getting over the sea wall and back with this thing anywhere else."

They set out together, each holding one handle of the barrow. They walked briskly, and the barrow bounced over the tufts of grass in the fields. They made for a point to the north of the little town, where a golf course had been made on the old sand dunes, built up by the sea before the wall was made. Here the landward side of the wall was a stretch of salty grass, sloping gently up to the parapet. Further north the landward side of the wall was steep, and there were few steps up and over it.

They reached Crossman's yard. This was an untidy cluster of boat sheds, and upturned boats occupying a grassy patch between the golf course and the wall. A rough road ran along behind the wall to it. Empty petrol cans, dented and rusty, lay around on the grass. A trawl net was hanging from a yard, waiting to be mended.

The boys took their barrow through the yard, and over to a wide gap in the parapet of the wall. From here a little wooden pier ran out across the beach. The tide was out now, leaving it high and dry, but at high water fishing boats from Rye and Dungeness could tie up here. Beside the pier was a slipway, shiny and green with the clinging plant life of the sea. The whole place looked neglected. It throve on the pleasure boats of holiday-makers, and this summer there were none.

As the two boys stood there, ready to wheel the barrow down the slipway a voice hailed them.

"That you, John? John Aston isn't it?" They turned. Crossman himself had come out of one of his sheds. He had a brown, tough face, with small bright eyes. He wore a dark blue sweater, rolled up to the elbow, and showing red and blue tattooing on his forearms.

"How is your father then? Have you come to look at the boat?"

"My father was well last time we heard, thank you," said John stiffly. He didn't like Crossman. When John's father was around, Crossman became almost fawning. Of course, Captain Aston had done a lot for Crossman, it was reasonable enough that he should be grateful; but there was something dog-like about his manner which upset John, and made him hate to hear Crossman even mention his father. But it would be nice to take just a look at the boat.

"Come and see her, Pat," he said. Crossman looked sharply at Pat, and let his eyebrows rise slightly. He led the way to the shed at the far end of his yard, and un-locked it with a huge bundle of keys. He flicked on a light, but the shed was still dark after the day outside. From the gloom the lovely shape of *Dolphin* leapt to meet John's eyes.

She stood on her launching trolly, prow towards them. She was fifteen feet long, and painted emerald green to the bulwarks, and white above. She had a small fore deck, then a cabin, and then a cockpit at the stern. The boys stood on tiptoe to look into the portholes. The cabin had two berths, and a little galley. The door from the cabin to the cockpit was on the port side, for the centre of the cockpit floor was occupied by the engine housing. Immediately behind the engine was the steering wheel, a good-sized one with a gleaming brass hub.

"My father designed and built her himself," said John. "He likes a wheel better than a tiller; he's used to an enormous wheel on his own ships. Do you know anything about boats, Pat? She's an unusual shape; Father thought she would be both stable and fast with it. We were going to take her down to Gibraltar this summer." He ran his hand gently over the paintwork.

"How should I know about boats, then?" said Pat. "I never seen the sea before till they dumped me down here, away from all me friends."

"Seems you have been making some more desirable friends since then," said Crossman's voice from behind them. He was still standing in the doorway. They had forgotten about him.

"Thank you, Crossman. She could do with dusting down a bit. See to it will you?" said John in a cold firm voice.

They marched out past him. Then they had to trundle the barrow down to the beach.

"You got everything, haven't you?" said Pat softly and bitterly. "You got just about the flipping lot!"

"No," said John quietly, looking up straight into Pat's eyes. "I don't think so. I haven't any friends. I can't seem to get to know people."

"Never mind," said Pat. "You got to start somewhere. Practise on a slob like me."

"All right," said John, "I will."

Pat grinned and started to shovel sand into the barrow. He said nothing more.

The barrow was nearly full, when suddenly the little

whisper of the waves fringing the sea far down the beach was broken by a deafening blaring, a klaxon sounding a wailing rising and falling note over the town. It was the siren warning of an air-raid. They looked at each other. They hadn't heard it often, and then it had twice been a false alarm.

"What'll we do? Run for a shelter?" asked John. The beach seemed suddenly horribly flat and exposed.

"Let's get under there," said Pat, pointing to the slip-way. It slanted down from the top of the wall to the level beach, supported on heavy, barnacle encrusted posts. They ran for cover underneath it. The siren stopped, and the waves took over again. Gulls called. There was silence otherwise. Pat pulled out his cigarettes, and offered John one, but he shook his head. Raids made him feel funny.

"I'll have to cut down on fags when we move up to your place," said Pat. "I'll be short on cash."

"Why?" said John vaguely, thinking of other things.

"Well, I keep myself in dough by pinching eggs from the farm. There's always some daft old hen gets out and lays in the hedgerow, instead of the boxes. Then if I gets there before that old cow of a farmer's wife, I nips them. The hotel buys them from me on the cheap. She knows I do it, but she can't catch me," he added, grinning.

John did manage to feel vaguely shocked, but he was much more conscious of the feeling air-raids gave him. It wasn't exactly being frightened. Of course it meant there was danger; but it was too impersonal, it threatened too many people, was too chancy, to make him feel scared for himself. Unless perhaps that tight feeling at the back of his throat, like the beginning of a sore throat, was fright. He definitely did feel solemn. He listened. There were only beach noises.

No; perhaps there was a very distant droning sound. Planes. This wasn't another false alarm. Both boys sat

40

still, straining their ears. There was a sudden volley of little cracking sounds. John couldn't bear not to look; Pat was already moving, and he crawled after him out of their damp shelter. They lay on the sand and looked out to sea. Far away, over the channel, they could see aeroplanes, flashing silver in the sun. They couldn't see what sort they were. They saw a line of scarlet sparks travel from one plane to the other; seconds later another string of little cracking sounds reached them. Then the anti-aircraft guns at the camp at Lydd joined in. The hasty banging from the near guns drowned the more distant ones. Then there was a plume of white smoke behind the foremost plane. Then there was a plume of black smoke; the smoke line curved sharply downwards; there was a flash of white foam on the surface of the sea; then nothing. The victorious planes were already disappearing to the north.

"Was it one of ours?" asked Pat.

"Can't tell at that distance. You know, if my brother had joined up, he would have been a pilot, most likely. He could fly. He learned while he was at University."

"Well, it isn't him in the drink, anyway."

"I don't think it was that sort of reason. I think he's as brave as most people. He just thinks it's wrong to fight, whatever the enemy does to you."

Pat thought for a bit. "That can't be true, though," he said. "I wonder if that was one of ours."

"No," said John eagerly, "I think he's wrong. But he says that to kill people you have to hate them, and it is always wrong to hate people. And imagine, if you thought that, what would you do?"

"Can't see myself thinking that. That ain't right." said Pat. "Come on. Let's get this filled up."

They went back to work. They had the barrow piled high and had pushed it up the slipway, gasping for breath, and got it half way through the boatyard before

41

the siren sounded the all-clear; a steady single note. It was a horrid noise but it was hard not to like it.

When they got the sand back home they found that the cement had not yet arrived. Pat returned to his bunk-building and John nailed some planks together to make boards, and fixed catches on the window frames to hold the boards, and black out the light from the windows. They wouldn't stop work at tea time; they took their tea in sips while they worked. By the time it got dark they were too tired to go on. Pat laid his tools carefully in a corner and went home. John went and sat with his mother, and fell asleep almost at once. He slept right through the news, but his mother said when she woke him to send him to bed that there had been nothing worth hearing in it.

Chapter Six

THEY continued to work at it the next morning. They were both tired of it now; John was stiff from the day before, and fed up with hard work. And he had done no Greek preparation for Mr Macleod's lesson that afternoon. But though they were fed up they kept hard at it, grunting amiably at each other instead of talking.

And they were making progress. Mrs Aston had found an old drum of whitewash, and John spent the morning slapping it on the walls, while Pat completed his carpentry, and cleared up. It all looked bright and clean, and surprisingly pleasant. Half way through the morning the cement was delivered.

Pat started mixing it at once. He made up half the load of cement with the barrow load of sand. It was hard work. He stood over the heap, lifting and turning it with a shovel, pouring more water into a well in the middle of it and lifting and mixing again. He had pulled off his shirt, and sweat glistened on his back. He made it much wetter than John would have expected; when it was ready it shook and trembled like a jelly, and Pat straightened, and leant against the wall to rest. He was broad in the shoulder, and his muscles made smooth bulges under his skin.

"Only bones show in me," thought John enviously, *"And I'd have to rest every half a minute doing a job like that."* And when he laid down his brush and went to help Pat spread the cement over the floor he found he could scarcely lift a shovelful of the stuff, and his admira-

tion for Pat's strength increased. There was skill as well as brawn in it. Pat spread the mixture out roughly over half the floor; then he got a wooden plank, soused it with water, and started smoothing the surface by slapping the plank up and down, drawing it little by little towards him. The cement shook, and made a watery noise under the plank. Slowly and reluctantly it settled into a smooth sheet. Pat spread some more and smoothed it, working towards the door. This time John took a turn. He wasn't much good at it, but between them they got it down over the whole of the first of the 'bedrooms'.

When it was done they both sat down. It was nearly time for lunch, there was no point in starting the other one.

"We need more sand," said Pat.

"I've got a lesson this afternoon. I'll help you get more when I get back."

"Thing is, that stuff takes twelve hours to set hard enough to walk on. Well, the old girl is off down to the clinic in the town to get herself weighed and that like, tomorrow morning. I thought perhaps we could move our things up here while she was out. But we'd have to do the other bit of floor today."

"Perhaps if we work late?"

"Couldn't you skip your lesson?"

"No," said John, "I don't think I could." But Pat, he suddenly remembered, had been skipping school all this time. It didn't seem to worry him. Yet he didn't try to change John's mind.

"Rightie ho, mate. See you when you get back. I've got to go off home for dinner today; she's beginning to wonder what the heck I'm up to."

"Bye then," said John.

In the kitchen he found his mother looking young and happy. Her face was glowing, and when she smiled at him she laughed a little. She had let the chops burn, and she said "Oh dear!" as though it didn't matter. The post had brought a letter from his father. His own heart bumped.

"Anything for me?" he asked.

"Lot's of love to Janjan." He didn't mind the nickname at all this time.

They sat down together, eating and talking. His mother propped the letter on the salt cellar, and read bits out to him. His father had reached New York safely. And now he had a fortnight's shore leave, while the ship loaded, and waited to join a convoy which was assembling for the voyage home. Captain Aston preferred to sail in a convoy, with some protection from the Royal Navy. And there was plenty of food in New York; he sent them the menu of a *five* course dinner he had eaten, and an account of a musical play he had seen on Broadway. And as always he reminded them not to forget their gas masks! They laughed as though this were a new joke, and Mrs Aston folded the letter carefully. She did not put it away, she kept it lying on the table beside her as they drank their tea.

Then John went to get his books, and set out for his lesson. It was another fine clear day. He walked along the sea wall, instead of going by the road. Mr Macleod's house was beside the golf course, and one could get there along the shore. Today there were ships in the bay. Ever since the war began there had been plenty of naval ships going up and down the Channel; but today there was something odd. A string of smallish ships was heading northwards up Channel, fairly near inshore. John looked carefully. A launch, unmistakably a Royal Naval vessel, had a bunch of very small craft in tow, perhaps a dozen of them, and was pulling them with her towards Folkestone. And just behind her was a steamer with a pleasure deck, and big paddle wheels amidships—the sort of thing which takes people for river trips. Whatever could it be doing on the open sea? It appeared to be following that curious Pied Piper of a launch.

John's lesson was very painful. So much using his muscles seemed to have dulled his mind. He had to confess to having prepared nothing, and Mr Macleod set him to translate unseen. The battle of Salamis ... a great victory for the Greeks. John imagined those narrow seas, very blue and sunny, and teeming with ships. Greek ships, rowed with banks of oars and painted with eyes at the prow. And the great Xerxes, sitting on his hill, watching his defeat.... It was a splendid story, but easier to imagine than to translate.

John stumbled over it, groping for words, getting stuck at things he knew well really. The Greek letters danced at him, and he misread them. Mr Macleod was angry. He became quiet and cold. When John blundered he winced.

"He loves this stuff," thought John. *"He can't bear to hear me murdering it. And only last week,"* he told himself in amazement, *"I thought this was important too."*

"Where's your head today?" exclaimed the exasperated tutor. "Now you just look at the text, boy, and follow while I construe."

He leant over John's shoulder, and pointed his finger at the words one by one. The muddled panorama of the sea-battle which had struggled through John's halting translation came suddenly into sharp focus in Mr Macleod's dry, clear voice.

"Xerxes, when he learnt the disaster that had occurred, fearing that an Ionian might suggest to the Greeks, or that they themselves might think of sailing to the Hellespont, to cut adrift the floating bridge; and fearing that he was in danger of being cut off in Europe, and perishing, decided he must run for it...."

"That's what will happen to us," thought John. *"'Cut*
46

off in Europe, and perishing.' The papers don't say it outright, but we are being pushed back and back, retreating, getting cornered, getting cut off in Europe...."

"Wishing that this should not be clear either to the Greeks or to his own people...."

"That's why the papers don't say. You can't say you are going to run for it. It mustn't be clear to the enemy, and it mustn't be clear to one's own people. It spreads alarm and despondency. We send people to prison for saying we might have to run for it. It makes everybody else feel like me now, alarmed and despondent...."

"He tried to complete the mole across the channel to Salamis, and he tied Phoenician merchant ships together, in order that they might serve as a pontoon bridge, and wall."

"'He tied merchant ships together' ... like the ships I saw just now tied together, going up the Channel. The channel to Salamis ... he put them across it to make a bridge. But you can't make a pontoon bridge across the English Channel. You could use the boats to bridge the Channel in another sense though...."

"John!" said Mr Macleod sharply, "Do you think I render this for my own pleasure? For the love of my own voice? You haven't heard a word of it!"

"I'm sorry, sir. I was listening. But I was thinking of something else as well. I saw something this afternoon that I didn't understand, and I understand it now."

"I'm glad indeed to hear it! And do you also understand your Herodotus? Bring me a written version of the whole chapter when you come next week. And good afternoon to you now!"

John thought ruefully as he hurried home that one result of doing very bad work was that one got off early. Half way back he met Pat, coming from the beach with a barrow full of sand, struggling along by himself. He was glad enough of John's help.

"You been hearing things, or is it just me?" he asked as they went.

"Not me. What things?"

"There, like that. There it was again."

He stopped the barrow, and they stood still. Faintly and muffled by long distance was a low-pitched rumble. The smallest nearby sound cut across it and extinguished it. But between the sound of a car on the Dymchurch road, and the crying of a gull on the shore, they could hear it, rumbling.

"What is it?" asked Pat.

"Guns I think. Far away," said John.

"But nearer than they were yesterday," said Pat grimly.

They had tea when they got back, and told Mrs Aston that they were going to do their best to finish the job that night, and move in in the morning.

"That's splendid!" she said. "I don't see why I shouldn't tell you both that I think you are very good, clever boys, with your hearts in the right place. I'm proud of you."

John grinned at his mother, loving to be praised by her, and then noticed that Pat had turned scarlet from his collar to his hairline, especially his ears, and that he didn't know where to look. Yet in spite of his discomfort, he looked pleased.

"I've made a chocolate cake for you to fill up with," said Mrs Aston. They ate nearly all of it.

John helped mix the cement this time. It was just as hard as it looked, and he wasn't very good at keeping the water in the middle of the mixture; it kept finding a gap and running out across the floor. It seemed ages till it was mixed smooth. And while they worked, silent, keeping their breath for the job, they heard that distant rumble again. It was a little different now—booms, coming a little while apart. A loose pane of glass in the

48

stable windows rattled at each one. They said nothing about it.

When the floor was finished they had a lot of odd jobs to do. John found a box of old plugs, wires, and electrical bits and pieces, and they rummaged in it for a fitting that would go into the socket in the ceiling. John's father never threw anything out; he seemed to have a sample of every sort of gadget since the beginning of electricity. After a lot of tries, climbing up the ladder and down again, they found a light-fitting to fit the rose. It looked fantastically old, and they both felt doubtful; but when they turned on the switch, and put a bulb in it, it worked.

They cheered loudly, and patted each other on the back. Then they found they could not turn it off; the ancient switch was stuck in the on position. They turned off the fuse in the cottage again, and tried to find a switch in the junk box. There wasn't one, but Pat understood electricity much better than John, and he used bits of several other things to fix one up. This time they cheered when the light went off.

It was late now, getting dark. Pat put his hand into his pocket for his watch. It wasn't there. He turned out all his pockets. They looked everywhere in the stable-house, and along the path to the kitchen door.

John went to find his mother. She was sewing again.

"Have you seen Pat's watch, mother? He had it in his pocket, because the strap's broken, and now he can't find it."

"Sorry dear, no I haven't. It won't be indoors, because I've cleared and swept the floor since tea. I'd have seen it."

"When did you last have it, Pat?" asked John. Pat was looking very miserable.

"I looked at the time on my way down to the beach. I haven't looked at it since."

49

"You didn't look at it on the beach?"

"No, but I did take out my handkerchief. And it was in the same pocket. I must have dropped it on the ruddy beach. And me Dad gave it to me. He hadn't any money to give me, see, so he give me his watch when he went off to the army. I'd wanted one ever so long." Pat was nearly in tears.

"Well," said John, pulling on his coat, "We'll just have to find it, that's all. And quickly before the tide comes up. Come along. We'll need a torch."

Pat went with him. They walked wearily towards the beach in the deepening darkness.

Chapter Seven

CLOUDS had come up with the dusk, and there were no stars and no moonlight. It was very dark. John knew the road so well that he could avoid the unevenness in the pavement without seeing, but Pat stumbled as they hurried along. When they reached the end of the made-up road, and started along the gravel path behind the parapet of the wall, John stumbled too.

They went through Crossman's yard and down the slipway. The sea sounded very near; their eyes accustomed to the gloom could pick out the white surf of the breaking waves only a few yards down the beach.

"I took the sand from over there a bit," said Pat. "There was some people sitting with a kid just here, so I went a little way along." They walked away from the slipway. But they could not see anything.

"Here!" said John. He had stumbled over some loose sand. They went down on hands and knees and ran their outspread palms over the bumps and hollows. They found nothing.

"We'll have to use the torch," said John. He flicked it on, holding it low, and shielding the light with his hand. They were searching a child's sand-castle.

"Things seem so different in the dark." said Pat. "It must be further over still."

They crawled along the beach, shining the half-covered torch ahead of them. Soon they found the scuffled sand and the hole, half filled with water now, where Pat had dug out the barrow load. They groped around, and shone the torch carefully, both of them hasty and uneasy, and without much hope.

"Hey, that ain't the west, is it?" said Pat suddenly. They looked up. The last light of the sunset had faded long ago, but there, far out over the channel, was a faint red glow, low down, like sunset where sunrise should be, and as they watched there came a brief streak of brilliant light across it.

"What is it?" asked Pat.

"Looks like something burning, doesn't it?" said John dryly. A little spasm of coldness squeezed his heart. He forgot that he was holding the torch, and let the beam glance sideways over a wider stretch of sand. Something gleamed in the light.

"There!" Pat pounced gratefully, and picked up his watch. John put out the torch, and they rose to their feet. For a minute they stood and gazed at the sinister red patch of sky over the distant shores of France. The sea was a great black void, edged by the sudden splashes of white of the waves. Dover light was faint with distance, but only four miles away the brilliant light of Dungeness still flashed out, and the Varne light out in mid channel sparked on the skyline opposite them. Their eyes travelled back to the eastern glow.

Suddenly there was the scratching noise of footsteps on the sand, coming from both sides of them at once, and a man thrust a gun up against John's ribs, and said sharply,

"Halt! Hands up. And no nonsense or I'll shoot!" John and Pat both put their hands up quickly. Then a gruff voice said "What's going on here?" A torch lit up the group of faces. There was a policeman standing beside Pat, and regarding John's assailant with the utmost surprise and suspicion in his round eyes.

"Ah, constable," said the gunman briskly, "Just help me to arrest these two men, will you? They are spies, dangerous customers, and probably armed. I have caught them red-handed, signalling to enemy shipping."

"Oh," said the constable warily. "Look more like boys to me. And if that's a gun you've got there you just put it down, and give me your name and address so I can check on your licence."

"What the devil do you mean?" shouted the other. "I'm a member of the Local Defence Volunteer Force, and this beach is my patrol area. You help me take these two back to Headquarters."

"We'll see about that. Have you got a licence for that gun? And I'll thank you to lower it this minute. Don't you know it's dangerous to point a firearm?"

"This is an outrage!" said the Local Volunteer. "Don't you know there's a war on?" But he lowered his gun.

"Now, then, you two," said the constable. "Who are you, what are you doing showing a light, why are you doing it, and where are your identity cards?"

"John Aston, and Pat Riley," said John, reaching into his pocket for his card.

"We were looking for my watch. I dropped it here this afternoon, and we wanted to get it before the tide came in," said Pat. He held out his card, very grubby and tatty. The policeman got out his own torch, and looked at them. "That's all right," he said, and handed them back. It was Constable Johnson, and he had known John for seventeen years, though he wouldn't admit to it on duty. "Get off now. Home to bed where you belong."

"No you don't," said the Local Volunteer, raising his gun. "You're under arrest, and you're coming with me."

"Now you look here," said Johnson, "You can't arrest people without a warrant, and you can't carry a gun without a licence, and you aren't taking these two any-where. If you try it, *I'll* arrest them for their own protection, and I'll take them down to the station, and have them driven home in a police car. Will that satisfy you?"

"But you surely don't believe them? I saw them signalling to enemy ships."

"Here you," said the constable in a weary tone of voice. "That watch you were looking for. Did you find it?"

Pat held it out to him. Both men looked at it. Damp sand still stuck to the broken strap. It looked very convincing.

"And where, may I ask," the constable demanded, "were you considering taking them?"

John suddenly realized that Johnson's hands were waving around as he spoke, in a sweeping gesture, in and out of the light cast by his torch. He was telling them to hop it. Pat saw it at the same time, and the two of them took two or three careful steps backwards, and then turned and ran.

"Halt!" came an angry cry, and then there were three loud bangs that left their ears tingling, and their hearts pounding. They dived under the framework of the slipway, where they had sheltered that morning. The pitch blackness swallowed them up. They scrambled right down to the bottom, where the sloping wooden ramp met the sand, and the sides were walled in, and they felt safer.

They had no sooner got there, trembling with fear and anger, than a blazing white light shone across the beach, and through the cracks in the boarding. Cautiously they crept forward again, and put their heads round the nearest post. The searchlight was shining from the top of the wall. It lit up the two figures on the beach, standing out brilliantly against the black night. The Local Volunteer held his gun pointing into the air; he had been firing over their heads. And the constable had taken out his notebook, and was writing in it.

John started to laugh. Perhaps it was the fantastic

scene; perhaps it was relief to see that the shots which had so scared him a minute before were in fact aimed at the sky. The laughter shook his whole body, and could not be suppressed.

"Shut up!" hissed Pat, and began to laugh also. They laughed together, stuffing handkerchieves in their mouths to muffle the noise.

Now a calm voice came from the source of the searchlight.

"I've got you covered. Come here slowly, and declare yourselves." The coastguards had arrived, and were taking charge of both the constable and the Local Volunteer. The argument continued on the wall beside the coastguard's light. The boys could see the Local Volunteer pointing to his armband, and the constable shaking his head. Then the great light was switched out, and the whole scene disappeared abruptly. It seemed that they all got into the coastguard's car, for a car started, and drove away, and then there was silence, except for the ceaseless sound of the breaking waves.

They sat and listened. John felt damp and cold sitting on the moist sand in the dank air under the green timbers. But he also felt very tired. His joints all seemed to be loose, and he ached a bit here and there. Pat must have felt the same, for he did not move either. Instead he leant back against a slimy post, and lit a cigarette. John could see only the little round red spark at the tip of it. He could hear a car approaching, some way down the road. Then when he stretched his legs out, his feet met an obstacle. There was a metallic thud, and a little slopping noise like water moving in a can, as something fell over.

"What on earth is that?" said John. Pat struck another match, and they looked. There were two blue two gallon tins sitting side by side near one of the frame posts. Pat's match burned out, and he lit another, and unscrewed the cap of one of the cans. A familiar smell reached their noses at once.

"Petrol," said Pat. "And it wasn't here this morning; we'd have seen it."

"Hey, what's that?" said John urgently. The noise of the car was very near now, and it was coming slowly. "They've come back to look for us," said John.

"Well let them look, then, I'm staying put," said Pat. They retired to the innermost corner of their hideout.

The car came very near, and then stopped. They heard footsteps. Someone was walking down the slipway over their heads, with steps that boomed above them. Then the steps paused and there was a soft scratchy thud; the approaching someone had jumped down onto the sand. The boys held their breaths. The outline of a man appeared in the gap between the frameposts; dark though it was outside it was still darker underneath, and they could just see him as an outline against the sky. Then he came in with them, and he was so close they could hear his breathing.

He breathed heavily, and he groped around in the darkness. Frozen with fright John held his own breath, desperately wondering what would happen if the stranger struck a match, or touched him, or Pat. The man found one of the tins, and they heard the petrol slopping around inside it as he picked it up. He fumbled around again, getting nearer and nearer. Trying hard not to make the slightest noise, John moved his leg, so that the groping hands would touch the tin before they touched him, and he closed his eyes in case the whites showed up in the dark. Another slopping noise told them that the second tin had been lifted; then the man grunted, and the sudden loud noise made John jump violently. He could hardly believe that the noise of his heartbeats thumping in his ears was not clearly audible to the intruder.

The man stopped for a few seconds, doing something else. Then he backed away and went. They heard his steps crunching on the sand; then he climbed onto the slipway, and walked to the top. They heard his car door softly closed, and then the engine started, and they listened to the rising note of the gear changes as the car drove away.

"Golly!" said John, "That was a near thing!" Pat was standing up, reaching for a pale square object left stuck between two timbers. It was a sealed envelope. He fingered it and handed it to John. There were some coins in it, and at least one note, for it crackled faintly too.

"Black market," said John. "If we'd have thought to look, I bet we'd have found that petrol was stained with industrial dye."

"Who do you think is working it?"

"It must be Crossman I should think. He gets petrol to supply fishing craft, and he probably has more than he needs now and then. He could easily leave it here for customers to collect, and from the feel of this envelope he gets well paid for it."

"What you going to do about it?" asked Pat with interest. "You going to tell him to be more cagey, or you going to turn coppers' nark, and give him away?"

"I don't know," said John. "I'll have to think. I think black marketeers are pretty rotten, but you see Crossman is a sort of friend of my father's."

"Lummy. Can't say I like his choice of mates!" said Pat feelingly.

They came out of their hiding place, and started to walk home. The sky had blown clear and there was a pale moonlight.

"Well, he's not a friend exactly. But he served on the same ship as Daddy once, and they got shipwrecked. Daddy came through all right, but they spent ages drift-

ing round in an open boat. It was the great war some-
time, and they had been sunk by the enemy, and they
were drifting around not knowing which side would
pick them up. Daddy says Crossman's nerve was broken,
and he's never been the same since. I think he's a nasty
customer, but Daddy says one must make allowances.
Anyway, he's helped Crossman quite a bit, and I think
he set him up in this boatyard. I know the land it's on
belongs to us. I don't think Daddy would be pleased
somehow, if I went to the police about Crossman. But I
still think he stinks!"

"I reckon it never does no good, having anything to do
with coppers," said Pat.

They were walking through Crossman's yard now.

"That's funny," said John, "*Sara Lou* has gone."

"Who's Sara Lou?"

"Crossman's biggest boat. He takes people from the
beach for trips round the bay in her in summer, from the
pier here. She's quite big; over thirty feet. She doesn't go
into any of the sheds."

"He must of sold her."

"I don't think he would, somehow," said John.

Chapter Eight

JOHN woke early the next morning. He lay in bed, looking at the faint hairline of light round the blackout
shutter on his window. He felt very tired; and yet not at
all sleepy. He heaved himself out of bed and opened the
shutter. A flood of white light poured into the room, still
pale from the newly risen sun. John looked back at his
crumpled bed with distaste, and plodded downstairs to
see what he could find to eat.

He found a slice of bread, and put margarine on it,
and covered it up with lashings of marmalade. Then he
switched on the radio. There was some light music. He
trotted round the cottage taking the blinds down, and
drawing the heavy, black lined curtains. The sunlight
rushed in, and lay in blocks on the floor, and slanted in
long bars across the dusty air. There always was dust in
the air for the sun to find. John watched the specks of
dust moving slowly, dancing, in their golden beam.

The day was full of a pleasant feeling that something
good would happen in it; of course, they would get Mrs
Riley settled. John had not seen her since the night
when he and his mother visited the railway carriage, and
he was surprised to find that the thought of helping her
pleased him so much. Yet he really hadn't given her a
thought while he was working on the stable; he had been
thinking only of the job in hand.

"This is a special announcement," said a grave voice,
cutting into the music on the radio. "We have just heard
from official sources that the forces garrisoning Calais,

59

after fighting gallantly against an overwhelming enemy attack, were forced to surrender last night. The town and district of Calais are now in German hands. Further news will be given as soon as it is received." There was a long silence, and then the music began again, jaunty, inappropriate.

John sat still. Fear, he remembered, from a lesson in biology in school, is a protective mechanism. Some chemical is pumped into the bloodstream, and it makes you feel like this, and produces the necessary action—usually flight. In the case of a chameleon, change of colour to match the surroundings; in the case of a hedgehog, rolling into a ball; in the case of soldiers, fighting back; in the case of young boys and women sitting at home in a country at war, no action is appropriate. But the chemical in the bloodstream, which does not understand this, continues to produce a feeling of acute discomfort, till action is taken.

He was trembling. When he noticed it he felt a wave of contempt. He set himself to stop, and in a few moments was still, and rigid in his chair. Then he determinedly ate another mouthful of bread and marmalade. He would be in the navy one day, able to fight back, he reminded himself. Then he stopped over the thought. He and Pat would be able to fight; his mother and Mrs Riley would always be in this horrible sitting-and-waiting trap. For women fear was always a thing to be suffered, never a thing to act upon. He was awed. It occurred to him for the first time that his mother was as brave as his father.

Then he let himself think about Calais, and face it properly. The guns they had heard yesterday, the flames in the distant sky reminded him how near it was. Doubtless the Germans could shell the English coast from there. And what about the Allied army? John went over to his map. He swept a handful of tanks and soldiers off the table, and they clattered into his box. The Allied line was cut in half; the north divided from the south.

Then he realized his mother was standing in the doorway, in her faded blue dressing gown.

"What are you doing, dear?" She came across and looked silently at the change he had made on the map. "The news?" she asked. He felt a sudden urge to protect her, to keep her from feeling fear.

"Don't worry, mother," he said, putting his arm round her. "Don't be afraid."

But, "I'm not afraid, dear," she said, quite kindly. "Let's make coffee, shall we?"

They ate breakfast quietly together, but his mother left *The Times* unopened beside her plate. John went upstairs to dress and make his bed, and came down again. He too shunned *The Times*, and took his Herodotus, and pretended to work.

Pat arrived at ten o'clock, having seen Mrs Riley safely onto a bus to go to the clinic.

"Come on, we haven't got long!" he said. "Let's take the barrow!"

They trundled it across the field. Really there was very little to take when you compared it with moving house; but it took them a lot of journeys just the same. They rolled up mattresses and the bedding, and tied them across the barrow with string. They piled china and pans higgledy-piggledy together in one rattling clattering load, and got it back with three cups broken. They brought the zinc bucket and the kitchen chairs, and then went back for the kitchen table. It was the hardest of all; it wouldn't go into or onto the barrow, and so they had to turn it upside down, and carry it between them all the way. They slung the clothes and oddments they had found across it, to save another journey.

When they got back with the table half the morning had gone. Mrs Aston came out with cups of coffee for

61

them, and helped them to arrange things. They put the table and chairs where they looked best.

"Now then," said Mrs Aston, "It's my turn. First, there's an armchair that used to go in the spare room, which just wouldn't fit anywhere in the cottage, so it got covered up and put in the shed. You can go and get that."

"Hooray!" said John, and off they went. It was big and heavy, and awkward to carry, and when they staggered back with it they found Mrs Aston with piles of cloth, all the sewing she had been doing, piled on the table.

"Go and get the rods for these, John," she said. "I bought them in town yesterday, and they are standing in the porch." John came back with a bundle of brass curtain rods. Mrs Aston sat down in the armchair, and directed the two of them like a general. Under her orders they unfolded, one after another, bright red curtains for all the windows, vast curtains to hang across the openings where the loose box doors had been, and make the bedrooms completely private, and covers for the bedding on the bunks. Pat fixed hooks for the brass rods, and John slid the rings onto the rods, and the two of them heaved the heavy curtains up into place. Another journey to the shed produced a battered cupboard for the kitchen things, and at Mrs Aston's suggestion they fixed rows of hooks in each of the bedrooms, and under the shelf in the kitchen.

"You know," said Pat, with a sudden hoarseness in his voice, "This is a sight nicer than what we've been used to."

"It wouldn't be hard to improve on that carriage, dear," said Mrs Aston.

"No, what I mean is, well, it's a lot better than anywhere what we've ever lived in!" He looked at his watch, and went off at a run. He had to meet the bus, and stop Mrs Riley from going back to the carriage.

"There are just a few things of yours to come over, too," said Mrs Aston.

"Things of mine?" said John, puzzled.

He followed his mother up to her room. There on her bed was a little wicker basket cradle with a pink fluffy cover, and a pile of tiny clothes, carefully pressed and folded, and smelling a little of moth-balls.

"Gracious, mother!" said John, "Whatever did you keep all this for?"

"Well, I thought I might find a use for it someday. And so I have. I expect Mrs Riley will be glad of it. You need such a lot of things for a baby."

"I'm only surprised you haven't found someone to give them to before."

"I haven't quite felt ready to give them away."

"Did you really put me in that pink thing?"

"I thought you might be a girl." Mrs Aston blushed slightly.

"Did you want a girl, mother?" This was the second surprising thought of the day.

"I'm glad I've got you, Janjan."

"Oh *don't* call me that!" But as they were carrying the cot downstairs he asked curiously:

"What would you have called me if I had been a girl?"

"Edith Angela." The names came off her tongue as though she had tried the sound of them often. But John roared with laughter. Edith! Really!

They put the cot beside Mrs Riley's bunk, with the clothes lying in it. Then they got a pot of geraniums from the porch, and stood it on the table.

"Come along," said Mrs Aston, "let's get back, and leave this bit to Pat. But just then they heard voices from outside.

"Look, Pat what is this? Don't you want any lunch?

It'll be ever so late!" Pat and Mrs Riley stood in the doorway.

"Do you know what he's up to?" said Mrs Riley, appealing to John's mother. But she just looked at John, smiling.

"We, er, found you somewhere better to live. Pat and I, and Mother of course," said John.

Mrs Riley was looking round the place with a blank, bewildered stare, seeing her own things there.

"Look, Mum," said Pat, almost shyly, and he switched on the electric light.

"And look here," said John, taking her by the arm to show her the kitchen.

"Tap works," said Pat proudly. "Come and look, Mum." He led her back to show her the bunks in their little rooms. Her face remained blank. The boys looked at each other, uneasy, longing for her to praise them, to say she liked it. Then Mrs Riley sat down in the nearest chair, put her face in her hands, and began to cry.

The most terrible look of dismay spread over Pat's face. John was horrified. Tears ran between Mrs Riley's fingers. Her shoulders shook. Then she took out a hand-kerchief, wiped her eyes, and looked up.

"Oh, Mum, don't you like it?" Pat almost wailed.

"And I thought you were getting into some awful trouble, going off by yourself like that! And all the while you was doing this." She dabbed her eyes again.

"What do you mean, you thought I was getting into trouble? What you getting at?"

"Playing truant from school, you been. Worried me sick it did. I thought you was going to turn out like your Dad, God help me. And now ... you're a good boy, you are, like your Dad in more ways than one." She turned to John's mother. "How am I going to thank you, and me with the baby coming," she said illogically.

"We are only sorry that we can't do better for you. I

didn't realize that this place could possibly be made fit to live in; you should have seen it a week ago. But our two boys have worked like slaves on it." She smiled happily at them both.

Mrs Riley got up. "You go and get that bag of shopping Pat, and I'll make you a spot of lunch. You must be hungry. Where did you put the kettle?"

"Come on, John, our lunch time too," said Mrs Aston.

They sat in their patch of sunlight in the kitchen, and ate a small chop, and a large pile of spinach each.

"Is your lunch all right, dear?" asked Mrs Aston.

"Fine."

"The greenstuff too?"

"What? Oh, all right. I'm not wild about spinach."

Mrs Aston coughed. "It's not spinach, dear, it's nettle leaves."

"You're joking," he said, looking at the remains on his plate in horror.

"No, I'm not, dear. The Women's Institute magazine is full of suggestions for making the best of 'Our Island Resources'; and one of them was eating nettles. Our poor old kitchen garden doesn't grow much else this year, so I thought I might as well try it."

"Well, you might have warned me before I ate it!"

"Come, Janjan, it wasn't too bad, was it?"

"I'll finish mine if you finish yours," he said grimly. So both plates were abandoned.

"We've missed the news," said Mrs Aston.

"Good!" said John rebelliously. "When we hear it it's always something miserable."

After lunch he took a deck chair in the garden. It was beautiful warm weather. He also took Herodotus. The heavy scent of lilac drifted across the garden, and bumble bees droned at him, but he couldn't feel drowsy, and he couldn't get his mind on his work. His gaze just bounced off the glaring white page. He got up and walked about the garden. It felt odd not to be working on the stable. He felt aimless, and bored. For a few moments he struggled to settle his mood by himself, and then he went to look for Pat.

Pat was sitting at the table, reading a book with a lurid picture of a scantily clad woman on the cover. His face expressed blank boredom, and he looked glad to see John.

"Trouble with this country dump," he said, grinning, "is that there's ruddy well nothing to do!"

"What do you feel like doing?"

"Well, I feel in the mood for the flicks. And fish and chips after."

"We could do that if we catch a bus to Hythe."

"I'm stony broke, mate."

"That's all right, I'm not. We'll have to hurry for that bus."

"I'm right with you," said Pat, seizing his coat. "Mum!" he yelled. "We're off. OK?"

"I heard you. Tata then. Bring us back cod and two fourpenny'orths for supper."

Pat took some money from Mrs Riley's purse, and they ran for the bus.

The bus ambled along the coast road. It was full of housewives out on a shopping spree. The sea sparkled blue, and the land shimmered green on either side. Soon they reached the Dymchurch wall, rising steeply from the road, and blocking their view of the sea. But not before John had noticed that there was once again a handful of small boats in the bay, making towards Folkestone. The bus rumbled along at good speed, for the road was flat. Then they crossed the Royal Military Canal, and passed a Martello tower, built to protect the coast against an invasion by Napoleon and now in use again, with an ack-ack gun mounted on it, and then they were in the town of Hythe.

The boys got off, and wandered up the town to the little cinema. The main picture looked fairly awful; all the stills on the posters were of passionate embraces; but there was a western and a newsreel with it. They bought a bag of sweets, and went in.

Being bored in the cinema is quite different from being bored in the garden. When you're bored in the garden, thought John, you feel useless and ashamed of yourself. But when you're bored in the cinema you feel superior, miles above all the fools, who actually *like* rot like this. He glanced at Pat, but to his astonishment Pat appeared to be watching attentively. As the sickly story wound its way through tearful partings and gushy meetings, John kept looking at Pat. Pat was with the film.

"I'd have thought he'd have more sense!" thought John, disgusted.

But when it was over at last Pat said, "Bit wet."

"You can say that again!" said John, unwrapping a toffee.

But he enjoyed the western. It was an absurd story about a stage-coach hold-up. None of the bad men could aim a gun; none of the good men ever wasted a bullet, they killed at every shot. John knew it was nonsense, but he liked it; especially the galloping horseback chases, of which there were a good many. But Pat kept eating sweets, and he looked bored now. Now and then he groaned softly at some turn in the story.

Then came the newsreel. Pictures of refugees; pictures of tanks and guns. Pictures of generals meeting and saluting. *Mr Churchill flies to Paris*; a picture of the Arc de Triomphe. A picture of ships at sea; the periscope of a U-boat bobbing in the circle of a telescope. A ship sinking, in flames. Tired soldiers marching. A house smashed by a bomb. An Anderson shelter in the garden of the house, not smashed. No lives lost. An elderly Jew, with white hair, and a little black skull cap, crawling in the gutter of a German street, with a placard round his neck, being kicked. A picture of Hitler.

The audience woke up. A derisive booing noise broke from them.

Then more pictures; the king in uniform. People in hats watching a horse race. Politicians going into the Houses of Parliament, and coming out of them. Then the cock crowing, and *God save the King* bashed out on a cheap theatre organ.

They filed out into the daylight. The crowd dispersed. Pat and John, finding that they had plenty of time till the next bus, wandered down to the sea-front, looking in shop windows, and looking for a fish shop. When they reached the harbour there was a little naval craft moored there, and some officers in uniform walking on its deck. They took another road back up into the town, and found their fish shop. Pat disappeared into the heavy odour of frying. He came out again with a bundle wrapped in newspaper to take home for supper, and two gently steaming greasy envelopes.

"Hope you like salt and vinegar," he said to John, handing him one. John looked at the warm envelope in his hand with embarrassed surprise. He had never eaten fish and chips from a shop in his life, let alone eating them in the street. To make matters worse, as they stood there they saw the bus coming, and ran for it. Pat settled into his seat, and ate his chips with every sign of appetite, and none of discomfort. Some of the passengers gave hostile stares in his direction. There was no doubt about it, Pat's bundle smelt fishy.

But John felt so awful already he could hardly feel worse, so he started to eat his bag of chips. They were very good, and he was hungry. *"What the heck,"* he thought to himself, and stared coldly back at the most disapproving passenger, until she sniffed and looked away. And he greatly enjoyed the rest of the bag.

"Makes you sick, don't it?" observed Pat after a bit, wiping his fingers on his handkerchief.

"What does?" asked John, startled, feeling full of chips. "Why eat them if they make you feel sick?"

"Not chips, dafty. That poor old Jew on the news."

"We'll stop all that when we win," said John. *"And we'll get it ourselves if we lose,"* he added to himself.

Chapter Nine

WHEN they got home they found Mrs Aston struggling with an axe and an orange box, trying to cut firewood. Her hair was falling into her eyes, and she looked flurried, but as though she were enjoying it.

"Here you are!" she said when she saw them. "Come and help. Get a fire lighted in that range in the stable, quickly. And a copper of water on to boil as soon as the fire is drawing."

"Right. What's up then?" said Pat easily.

"The baby's coming," said Mrs Aston, making for the stable. "You got her moved up here just in time!"

John took the axe, and chopped up the box. Pat stood rooted to the spot, looking green.

"Snap out of it!" said John crossly, putting the firewood into Pat's arms, "and get going!" He went to find a scuttle of coal. When he came back with it Pat was standing in the stable door, asking John's mother, "Is she all right? She going to be all right?" But when they went in Mrs Riley was sitting in the armchair drinking tea, looking just as usual.

"Blimey. Thought you was having a baby then," said Pat indignantly.

"I'm waiting for you to get a fire going, that's what," she said. Pat grinned broadly at her. They went into the kitchen and started to pack the grate in the range with squashed up newspaper, and bits of wood. Then they tipped coal on top and set a match to it. Thick choking smoke billowed out into the room. They coughed and spluttered.

"Chimney's blocked," cried John in dismay. "We forgot to sweep it."

"Didn't need it, I looked," replied Pat. "Try putting the lid on, dafty."

John replaced the round lid over the stoking hole, and closed the front of the fire. There was a deep roaring sound as the draught pulled the sparks into flame. The boys found the zinc bucket and stood it in the sink under the tap. The tap ran sluggishly and the bucket took a long time to fill.

While they stood there, there came a sharp ratatat on the door, and a grey-coated nurse came in with a large black bag. She took a quick look round the room, and glanced into the bedroom.

"Yes, yes, this will do very nicely. I can manage quite well here. You need not call an ambulance, you can leave the hospital beds for those who really need them." She took off her coat as she spoke, and put her bag on the table. Then she looked up and saw the two boys.

"Out," she said. They went.

In the cottage everything seemed empty and quiet. The kitchen clock ticked loudly at them. On the table lay the bundle of fish and chips they had brought back from Hythe. It steamed feebly at them.

"I don't think I could," said John, "Let's make omelettes."

"Speak for yourself," said Pat tipping half the contents of the parcel onto a plate. He looked ruefully at the rest. "Do you think the old girl might feel like this later?" he asked.

"Crikey, *I* don't know!" said John. The whole question of what Mrs Riley might feel like was beyond him. Then he looked again at the limp chips lying in the blotchy greaseproof paper, and decided that after all he could cope with the question. "But I should think it highly unlikely," he said decidedly. His omelette stuck to the pan, and burnt.

Nevertheless, they both sat down bravely to their supper. John ate lots of bread to mask the burnt taste. They made a pot of tea to finish off with.

"How about *them*?" asked Pat when John brought two tea cups from the cupboard. He inclined his head in the direction of the stable.

"Couldn't do any harm to offer, could it?" said John. He poured four cups, and stood two of them on a tray. "Who's taking them?"

"Not me!" said Pat. So John went. He knocked on the door, and his mother called, "Who is it?"

"John, with cups of tea." She came to the door and took them.

"Bless you dear," she said, closing the door again.

John went back to drink his tea with Pat. He glanced at the clock, and turned on the radio for the news. The grave voice announced to them that King Leopold of the Belgians had surrendered to the enemy. The Belgian army had withdrawn from the fighting. The German advance continued. John felt his throat tighten. His stomach sank as though he were standing in a lift.

Pat stared at him. His face became blank. "That bad, then?" he asked. John nodded. He remembered how he had got it all worked out, there was nothing for him to do about any of it; he just had to feel scared and put up with it. Unless...

Pat interrupted his train of thought, by suddenly exclaiming. "Makes me sick it does! I don't see what's going on. You listens to the news, and reads your paper as though you knew what's what. Me, I don't know a thing. I don't even know where these ruddy places are. Just words it is to me. If Jerry knocks me off with a bomb, I'll be the only corpse in England as doesn't know why. Ruddy awful, that's what it is. You're scared too; I can see that. But you got something to be scared about. Me, it's like being scared in the dark." He stubbed out his cigarette viciously. "Sorry, mate," he said after a pause. "Shouldn't of blowed me top. Not your fault."

"Perhaps it is. What do you want to know? If it's anything I know, I'll gladly tell you."

Pat relit his cigarette. It was the last one in his packet. John went into the living-room, on a sudden impulse, and got one for himself from the box his mother kept for visitors. He felt more companionable, holding one too, but he forgot to light it.

"What I want to know is, what will happen if Hitler wins?" said Pat.

"He won't win."

"No, I don't mean that. I know he won't win, I mean what will happen if he does—what are we fighting to stop? I can't say any better, I'm not good with words like you, but you see what I'm getting at?"

"I think so. Well, I'll do my best. Hitler has power in Germany. He doesn't share it like people do here. So nobody can stop him doing what he wants to. And some of the things he wants to do are horrible; he thinks the Germans are the master race, and ought to lord it over Europe, and he persecutes Jews and Gipsies, and all sorts of people just because of their race. He'll do the same in any country he conquers; Holland and Belgium now, and France next, and then probably us, if he can. So we have to fight to stop him if we want to be free to live decent lives."

"Well, I get that anyway. But what I don't see is, what does he get out of it?"

"Lots of power, that's all."

"He must be nuts! "

"Perhaps. It's a nasty form of madness."

73

"And he's winning?"

"He's just smashed the Belgians, and that leaves us in a mess. Come and look." The two boys looked at John's map. John found it was a relief to explain to Pat. Somehow saying it all aloud was better than having unspoken fears all the time. He pointed at his map.

"We were holding a line about here. The French were on our right in the south, and the Belgians on our left, in the north. The Germans struck through here, and took Calais. That leaves quite a few French, and ourselves, and the Belgians cut off from the rest of the allied armies further south. And now the Belgians have surrendered, and are retreating. That opens up this flank, like that!" John pushed the soldiers back across the map. "And it leaves us suddenly exposed to attack from the north. With no way out."

"Aren't we fighting for the Belgians? What stinkers to rat on us like that!"

"They probably can't help it. And it's hard to tell what the real situation is; they can't put everything in the newspapers. It would help the enemy. So we only know roughly what's going on."

"And how do you know all this? Just reading the papers?"

"Well, yes really."

"It must be the posh papers. The ones I read don't seem to do it."

"Let's have a look at today's now," suggested John. He thought he ought to keep Pat's mind off what might be happening in the stable house. They spread *The Times* out on the floor, and lay stretched out side by side to look at it. They skipped through the military news; it was already out of date.

"Look," said John. "Here's that raid we saw yesterday. 'Sirens sounded, and ack-ack engaged off the Kent coast yesterday'." It didn't tell them whose plane had gone down. They scanned the closely printed columns for news. The first civilian casualties of the war were reported; eight people injured in a north-eastern town. The Post Office was accepting gifts of books and magazines to be distributed to the forces. Four hundred thousand people had been enrolled in the Local Defence Volunteer Corps. More were to be enrolled from the age group eighteen to nineteen and a half.

"Oh, well, not quite so long to wait before we can arrest spies on the beach ourselves," commented Pat. "Hey, look at this... 'The following areas are declared evacuation areas: Yarmouth, Lowestoft, Felixstowe, Harwich, Clacton, Frinton, Southend, Margate, Ramsgate, Sandwich, Dover, Deal, Folkestone.' That's almost here! No sooner get me Mum settled than they start moving us all out again!"

"Not quite," said John, reading on. "'Broadcasting last night Mr Macdonald said that the new areas were confined to urban areas on our coasts which are closely populated. For the present there was no need for any but these towns to be added to the places for which evacuation is planned'."

But it still looked bad. Was it shelling from the Continent they were afraid of? Surely not. Bombing? Why specially coastal towns? But if it was invasion they were thinking of....

John hastily turned the page, and they looked at the letters to the editor. There were a lot of angry letters about which weapons Local Volunteers should carry, and whether they should be controlled by the military authorities. Someone suggested that evacuees might well have spies among them; they were far from home, and nobody knew who they were anyway. They should all be carefully watched.

"Haha!" said John. "I always thought you had a German accent, Pat!" Pat punched him in the ribs.

Another letter suggested that German parachutists and spies would be greatly hampered if all signposts were taken down and all names of places removed from shop signs, station platforms, street names, and other public places. Then anyone who was seen opening a map could be arrested.

They read open-mouthed; then they both started to laugh. They imagined an England full of lost motorists, mislaid lorries, passengers alighting in the wrong places, parcels and vans searching vainly for addresses. They laughed till they felt weak.

"Well, all the loonies don't read the crummy papers!" said Pat at last. Then he sat up. "But really, John, I don't see that any of that gets us much further. I mean, none of that seems to matter very much." He got up, and looked at the map.

"My Dad's over there somewhere," he said. "What's it like for him, do you think? What are they doing there?"

John came over and looked too. He didn't need to.

"I suppose they might be trying to fight their way through to join the armies in the south."

"But you don't think so?"

"No. I don't know anything about it, but it seems to me they must be trapped."

"What will happen to them then?" Pat's voice was very quiet.

"They might have to surrender—but, look, Pat, do you know what I think? I think they're pulling them out, all they can."

"Bringing them home?"

"Yes, look. They haven't got much coastline, but there is a port there—Dunkirk. I've been there once; there's a proper port, with two long piers. Men could embark there. And it's obvious, isn't it, that we are in a real spot if our army is captured, but if we could get them out they could fight again."

"Poor blighters," said Pat softly. "Why isn't it in the papers then?"

"That would just be asking the Germans to bomb and shell Dunkirk, wouldn't it? Not that they need any asking, I dare say."

Pat said slowly, "They couldn't all get away, could they? Some of them would have to hold off the Germans, while the rest hopped on board."

"Yes. And it isn't so easy to 'hop on board', as you put it. There are hundreds of thousands of them, and it would take days for them just to walk up the gang planks. And the port will be under heavy bombardment, and so will the ships. It must be hell on earth."

"You mean, there's lots of them what aren't going to make it?" Pat was speaking evenly, controlling the tone of his voice; John, deeply excited, spoke urgently and fast.

"No, I mean I think they haven't a hope of getting everyone out through the port. I think they must be taking them off the beaches. In fact I *know* they are.... I've seen things. Yesterday, and today, there were boats in the Channel. Little ones. Pleasure steamers and small craft. The navy had dozens of them in tow. And then that boat has gone from Crossman's yard. And the fishing fleet has just disappeared. The weather is beautiful, and they aren't out fishing the bay, and I haven't seen any of the men lounging around ... they've just gone somewhere. Well, look Pat, you don't need little boats to get men off a pier; but what if you have to get them off a beach? The water would be too shallow for big ships to get near in. And suddenly, the navy are taking small boats...."

"You mean," said Pat incredulously, "that our men will be standing around on the beach, like a picnic, waiting for a lift?"

"Yes. But no picnic. Being fired at and shelled all the time."

"It's flipping well crazy!"

"We've lost you see. It's always hard to organize a retreat."

"How many of them will get off?"

"I don't know. It will be a miracle if we get half of them home, I'd say. I don't know."

"And the others?"

"They'll have to surrender in the end."

"Cripes," said Pat softly. "Just standing on a beach, looking at the sea, and waiting, and waiting, and then getting caught."

"Yes." John was cold inside. Fear had stiffened every nerve of his body, and was squeezing the breath in his throat. But it was not the "Here-I-sit" fear this time.

Pat was saying: "You think the fishing boats have gone to get some soldiers. The crews have just got in their boats, and gone ... just like that. Blimey, that's something for you! That must take nerve!"

"Have you got nerve, Pat?" John's voice was thick, as though he were clearing his throat.

The dusk had come down outside, and the light in the room had dimmed and thickened round them. Pat turned to look at John, but John could not see his face clearly. He did not answer at once. John looked steadily at him. If he would not help, then it would be impossible. They could stay here safely. Except that nowhere was safe any more. It only came down to choosing between two sorts of fear.

"I got as much nerve as you, I reckon," said Pat at last. "So what?"

"I could take my boat, and go and help. But it takes two to handle her for a long trip really. It would be safer, more sensible with two..."

78

"Count me in," said Pat. "How are you going to do it? Where you going to get juice for her?"

John had worked it out. "I'm going to tell Crossman that we know he's trading on the black market, and that we'll tell the police, unless he gets *Dolphin* launched and ready, with her tanks full, for the first tide tomorrow."

Pat whistled. "You ain't as soft as you look," he said. There was only admiration in his tone as he added, "That's blackmail!"

"I think it will work. I don't think Crossman's got much guts. But look, Pat, I can't let you in for this without warning you. We might get killed. In fact we'll probably get killed. Nobody will be defending us. It couldn't be a more dangerous thing to do. But England isn't short of boys like us; she is short of trained soldiers." The warning he honestly intended had turned into an appeal. But he couldn't have felt more certain that what he proposed was right; a good, a splendid thing to do.

"Cut out the speeches," said Pat. "We ain't no use here; we might be a bit of good there. Worth a try. You going to talk to Crossman now?"

"Right away."

"I'll come too."

John wrapped his striped school scarf round his neck, though the feeling of cold probably came from inside rather than outside. And they went.

Chapter Ten

CROSSMAN lived in a tumbledown shack at the back of his yard. A slit of light was showing round one of the windows. John knocked sharply at the door. After a little while Crossman opened it. He looked surprised.

"Good evening, Crossman. May we have a word with you?" said John.

"Come in," said Crossman. The boys stepped inside.

"Do you know there's a light showing round your shutter?" John asked. They stood looking round while Crossman adjusted his blackout arrangements. The place was not at all tumbledown inside. It was spick and span, everything clean, and neatly arranged. There was only one room; it had a sink and stove at one end, and a bed at the other. A fire burnt in the grate, and an arm-chair was pulled up near it. Over the bed hung two pictures, one of a ship, one of three rows of sailors like a school photograph. To John's great surprise and annoyance, he saw propped on a little chest a picture of his father in uniform. He remembered that Crossman always said his father had saved him in that shipwreck, and his father always denied it.

Crossman was looking at him now, enquiringly, not displeased at a personal visit. "I put a rag over *Dolphin's* paint, as you asked," he said. He started to fill a pipe, and he kept his eyes on John.

"Thank you," said John. "I would like you to do something else for me please." Out of the corner of his eye he saw Pat lounging, hands in pocket, against the wall, watching.

"I'm always glad to be useful to any of your family," said Crossman.

"I want you to get *Dolphin* ready for a trip. I want her launched, with everything checked, and her tanks filled up, as early as the tide allows tomorrow."

Crossman's expression changed abruptly. His eyebrows lifted. "Might I ask where you could be going? You know how dangerous it is to take boats out, with mines everywhere, let alone U-boats. You'll have to do without your cruising this year, son."

"We are going with the others," said John quietly. His voice was steady, but he had started to tremble. "To Dunkirk or thereabouts. Where that boat of yours has gone."

Crossman turned round, and bent his head, lighting his pipe, and presenting his back to them. "Not with my help, you aren't," he said at last.

"I think you had better do as I ask you," said John. His voice was cold and even.

Crossman turned to face him. "Look, son," he said. "This is no kids' game. You are right about what's going on; but you haven't any idea what it is like. You would be sailing into the middle of a battlefield. They are taking men off from right under the nose of enemy guns; sitting ducks those boats will be, and no defending them possible. Let me tell you, it isn't funny being under fire. And in a boat it's worse; fire and water, either will kill you. Have you ever thought of dying, son? Really dying? Or getting your face smashed in? Have you considered losing your legs, or losing your eyes? Have you ever seen a man who's been wounded badly? I have. I saw enough in the last war to last me for as long as I've got to live. You think about it, and go back home to bed."

"I see why *you* haven't gone with your boat," said

John, steady resolve showing in the tone of his voice. "But that's your own affair. I didn't ask you for advice. I asked you to get my boat ready."

"Sorry son, but I won't do it. I'll tell your Dad you thought of it; shows pluck."

The assumption of superiority, the tone of a grown man speaking to a child made John feel silly and helpless, but it also made him angry. And he could see that Crossman was shaken; afraid even. He was afraid because John and Pat were ready to do what he himself had shrunk from doing. It was really they who were strong, and Crossman who should be patted on the back and sent to bed. John braced himself as though he were going to take a dangerous jump. He glanced at Pat.

"You will do just as I say, Crossman," he said firmly, "because if you don't I will go to the police with evidence that you have been trading petrol on the black market."

Crossman's gaze did not shift from John's face. His expression did not change.

"You wouldn't do it," he said at last. "You wouldn't do a thing like that. You know I'd be finished at this job if they stopped me selling petrol; and you know your father set me up here. What would *he* think if you did a thing like that?"

But now John had won. "What would my father think of you, do you think, if he knew you were using the job he found you to sell petrol to crooks? Lining your pocket out of the petrol that he risks his life every day to bring here? Shall I tell him, or will you get my boat ready?"

Crossman turned his back on them again. Then he said. "I'll have her ready. But you get out of here! Get out of my place!"

They went. Excitement, and the sheer strain of imposing his will on another person had made John tremble from head to foot the whole time he had stood in Crossman's room. Now he felt weak and tired.

"You're quite something, when you gets going!" commented Pat, admiringly.

"We ought to get home, and get some sleep," said John.

When they got home, Mrs Aston was sitting, hastily eating some supper.

"The midwife is very nice and capable," she said. "But Mrs Riley seems to like me there, so I'll get back as soon as I've had some coffee. You'd better stay the night over here Pat."

Left alone once more the boys pondered.

"Have you got boots, Pat?" asked John. It turned out that Pat hadn't any suitable clothes. They went upstairs, and clambered into the loft in which all the contents of boxes and cupboards from the other house had been crammed. John found a pair of his father's sea-boots, a bit big for Pat, but wearable. Then he found his own. Then he found a duffle coat, and an oilskin cape. There was only one sou'wester, but among the folded things in one wooden box he found an old officer's cap belonging to his father, and a blue jacket with gold braid. They were rather loose on him, but they would do. They carted the clothing downstairs, and then John rummaged through the drawers of a tallboy in the living-room, looking for a chart of the Channel. He found one much battered by use.

"I don't think we'll need this," he said. "Not if there's as much going on as there has been today. We won't know where the minefields are, so we will have to try and follow someone who knows more than we do; but a chart is a good thing to have, just in case."

While he searched around, Pat, with nothing to do, sat in the armchair, staring at the pattern on the carpet, and looking tense. John put a hand on his shoulder.

83

"You go to sleep now, Pat. We'll make up the camp bed for you."

"Don't think I could sleep, thank you. Me gut's all knotted up. I'll sit here."

"You'll go to bed, and sleep! I'll get you some aspirin and a hot drink, that helps. Captain's orders."

Pat grinned stiffly. "OK," he said.

When John had settled Pat he went up to his own room, carrying a mug of hot cocoa. Suddenly a flood of affection for the room came over him. He looked at the bright blue bedcover, the little wicker chair, the round picture of his grandmother mounted on black velvet, the ship in a bottle, that his father had brought for him when he was very young, and all these things seemed heart-warming, dearly loved, safe and inviting. How comfortable his bed looked! But he didn't get into it at once. He got into his pyjamas, and then sat in his chair, opened his writing case, and took a clean sheet of paper.

Dear Mother, he wrote, *I have gone.* Then he crossed that out and wrote, *Pat and I have taken* ... Then he crossed that out too, and threw away the piece of paper. He sat thinking. How could he put it, so that she would not be worried about him? There wasn't a way of doing that. She would be terrified. For the first time John wondered whether it was, after all, a noble thing to do. But then, if everyone stayed at home for their mothers' sakes, Hitler would have the world for himself. And then John had begun to learn that his mother wasn't as delicate as she looked. She never fussed about his father.

But still, it was hard to think of a way of putting it. Perhaps he ought to say they had gone fishing for the day, or something like that. Then they would be back before she began to worry. Or would they? Just how long was it going to take? John realized with a lurch of his stomach that it was impossible to imagine being back; his mind wouldn't do it. It ran ahead only as far as getting there, and then it absolutely stopped. He didn't believe they would ever get back. He shook himself, and gulped some chocolate. He was being a fool. Of course they would get back, and they had a good chance of getting some soldiers back with them. That was the point of going. It was just that it was so tremendous that it filled his mind. He couldn't imagine doing anything ordinary, like going off for his Greek lesson, ever again.

No, he couldn't tell a straight lie to his mother. He couldn't even write *Don't worry*. He wrote, *Back as soon as possible, love, John*. He put the note on his chest of drawers, and climbed into bed.

Chapter Eleven

THE little alarm clock woke him at six o'clock. He was wide awake on the instant, his mind clear. He slipped out of bed and down the stairs to wake Pat. But Pat was awake already, lying looking at the ceiling with very open eyes. He got up as soon as he saw John.

"Get dressed," said John, and went upstairs to dress himself. On the way he saw through the landing window that the midwife's bicycle was still leaning against the stable wall.

He put on old trousers, a shirt, a scarf instead of a tie to keep the sharp sea air from blowing down his neck. He tried his father's jacket, and decided against it. It was uncomfortable. He found a thick ribbed dark blue sweater instead. Then he picked up his boots and his father's cap, and tiptoed past his mother's door.

The door was open. He could see his mother fast asleep, curled up like a child, with the blankets pulled up to her chin. He would have liked to go and kiss her, but he smiled at her instead, and very gently closed her door. Then he went downstairs.

Pat was dressed. John looked at him critically, and then found him a scarf to tuck round his neck.

"Mmm. You'll do," he said.

"We ought to fill up with grub, but we can't cook bacon; the smell might wake your mum. What is there?" said Pat. They looked in the larder. Porridge seemed to be the best bet. Pat made it, while John searched for more. He found a tin of corned beef, and a tin of peaches. They put the peaches on top of their plates of porridge, and ate the corned beef with bread as a second course. When he went to the larder to fetch the margarine for the bread, John saw the second half of his week's butter ration, standing in a little dish. His mother wouldn't let him touch the second half till Thursday; but then, he thought, he mightn't be here on Thursday, and it would be a dreadful pity to waste it. The thought of not being here didn't disturb him in the least this morning; he had got used to it. But he took the butter. He and Pat shared it, spread gloriously thick, smooth and melting in their mouths. They drank plenty of hot coffee.

"Seems a bit mean to leave the washing-up," said John, "but I think we'd better go." They stacked the dirty plates neatly on the draining board, just to show willing.

"Put on that oilskin," said John to Pat as he put his duffle coat on.

"You're joking; the sun's coming up. Lovely morning it is."

"Wear it just the same. It's important not to get cold. It will be cold at sea, and it's much easier to stay warm than to get warm again after you've got cold." Pat made a face at him, and did as he was told.

It seemed odd to John that for once he was the one who knew more about practical details. But of course, he had grown up with boats.

They closed the kitchen door, and walked quietly past the stable, wondering in silence how Mrs Riley was getting on, and took the path to the sea. It was a cool misty morning, with that gold tinge to the haze which means it will be clear and warm later on. There was nobody about. Once they heard a distant chink of milk churns being moved on one of the farms, but they did not see the dairyman, and it gave the day a feeling of something

87

new; something not handled, not breathed, by anyone before them. Lots of little things were happening. A bright globe of dew ran down a slanting blade of grass, to disappear in the general moisture of the ground. A bird hopped three times one way, and twice another, and cocked his head at them before flying off. They heard his wings. Sheep bleated mournfully from nearby fields.

Then they reached the wall, and walked along it, and the world looked different. The sea is always fresh, always empty. A great blank sweep of sky, a great flat plain of grey water, filled up the view, all without detail, all vast. Only the wind happened to anything here, and the myriad featureless wrinklings of the surface of the sea.

The tide was high, and the wind coming off the sea was cold. John shuddered. Crossman was standing in his doorway, waiting for them. He looked tired and harassed. Looking down at the sea, the boys saw *Dolphin* ready launched, tied up to the little pier. She looked quite a different shape in the water—much smaller.

"I've got some things to give you. I've not put them aboard; you mightn't find where I'd stowed them. Will you step inside?" said Crossman. The boys followed him in.

Crossman's table was covered with carefully laid out things.

"Take stock of what's here, and remember where you stow everything when we take it aboard," he said. "Blankets; only two, I haven't more. Food; biscuit and guava jam, army stores stuff. Not tasty, but filling. And two pounds of chocolate. I've only one thermos flask; here with coffee in it. But I've made some soup, and put it in these stone bottles. I'll show you where to put them under the engine covers so that the engine will keep them warm."

"We aren't lifting a siege!" exclaimed John, astonished.

Crossman turned to look at him levelly. "That's just about what you are doing. I've been in this sort of shambles, I tell you. Any men you pick up will be cold and hungry, and you'll need to eat yourselves. Keep this stuff, don't eat it all at the beginning. Now look here; this is a box of bandages, and iodine and such like. Aspirin here. This ointment for small burns—a bad burn shouldn't be touched. There's a pair of scissors too. Twenty cigarettes; I can't spare more. And last thing, this." He brought from his cupboard a hip-flask of brandy. "One of you wear this. Don't let a tired soldier get it unless he needs it. *Dolphin*'s in good order. I've filled her main tank, and her reserve tank. I think it would be dangerous to carry spare tins in the cabin." Crossman stopped. He looked more tired than before. "I can't think of anything else I can do for you," he said. "Give me a hand carrying this lot."

They walked over the planking of the little pier, laden with all these things. John stepped easily across the gap between the gently bobbing boat, and the solid pier, and Pat and Crossman handed things down to him. He put the food in the galley, stowed the jars of soup against the warm part of the engine under Crossman's instructions, and put the first-aid stuff under one of the bunks.

"You've got enough petrol to keep going till to-morrow night some time," said Crossman. "If you don't keep switching her on and off. You shouldn't have to. Don't forget to bail out. I've stowed a pair of oars under the port bunk in case the engine packs up. God help you if that happens." He took Pat's hand to steady him as he jumped on board. Pat made the jump clumsily, and *Dolphin* tilted sharply under his weight, and then rocked back the other way equally sharply. Pat sat down abruptly on the bench that ran round the cockpit.

"All set," said John. He looked up at the man standing on the pier. "Thank you, Crossman," he said. There was no coldness in his tone now. He started the engine. It spluttered, and then chugged gently. Crossman cast off, dropping the painter onto the foredeck with expert hand. John eased *Dolphin*'s nose away from the pier, let out the throttle and took her seawards. He turned to wave at Crossman, but he had turned his back, and was walking home. Then he increased the speed till the foaming water curled up proudly round *Dolphin*'s bows, and they were off.

He set a course not too far out to sea, for he planned to follow the coastline round the curve of the bay of Folkestone. There were no ships in sight to follow, but at Folkestone something would surely be happening. They passed the water tower at the very end of the town, and now they could see nothing of the land except the wall. The morning mist still wreathed the hills beyond the marsh at Hythe. There was a light swell, enough to make *Dolphin* feel alive under John's feet. He loved the feel of the sea, and he was rejoicing now at the graceful movement of his boat.

"What'll I be doing now?" asked Pat. Something in his voice made John look at him sharply. He looked a funny grey colour.

"You all right?" said John.

"Fine," said Pat shakily.

"Well find your way around first. Go and look at the primus in the galley and make sure you can work it. And practise walking without lurching, and then you can climb round the cabin to the foredeck, and get used to doing that." Pat took a wide-eyed look at the cat-walk round the cabin, and disappeared inside.

He was gone a long time. John kept *Dolphin* running smoothly. He wanted to give Pat a chance to find his sea-legs before he took her up to full speed. He remembered his father's voice, crying out to his mother, who liked this moderate speed, "Ah, let her *rip!*" How much less worrying it would be, he thought, if his father were here with him.

Pat appeared again. He looked terrible. He looked at the narrow foothold round the outside of the cabin, and shuddered visibly.

"You hold the rail round the cabin roof!" John called to him. Pat did so; he more than held—he clung. Moving painfully slowly he struggled along and went out of sight round the cabin. John held the wheel lightly. He could feel the tilt of the boat caused by Pat's movements. Then he saw Pat lean out over the rail, doubled up with sickness. He hung there for what seemed ages to John. Then he scrambled back. He still looked grey, but slightly less miserable.

"Go inside and lie down," suggested John.

"No thanks," said Pat bravely. He sat down in the cockpit, and watched the coast go by. "The water comes awful near the top," he said after a while.

"She does ride rather low; but the hull is scooped to throw the wash outwards when she goes fast."

"You mean she goes faster than this?"

John laughed, and gave *Dolphin*'s horse power its head. The engine tone rose; a great scroll of white water rolled past her on either side; a long white trail washed out on the sea behind her. The air on their faces grew into a wind, and the joy of speed in wide places lifted John's heart.

"Coo!" said Pat.

"Go and eat a biscuit if you can bear the thought; it will settle your tummy a bit."

Pat scowled at him, and went to get one. John wondered how bad Pat did feel. It hadn't occurred to him that Pat might be sea-sick; and it wasn't just that. Pat was scared, scared of being in a small boat. John could have kicked himself for not realizing a complete land-lubber would feel like that. It was disturbing; John needed Pat to take the wheel part of the time. He had reckoned on being able to show him the works in these quiet coastal waters, but it wouldn't do while the poor fellow felt as sick as that. Of course, Pat was being very plucky about it ... but there was far worse to come. John's father had told him once, talking about Cross-man, that courage wasn't something you always had lots of, or always had none of; courage was like water in a bucket—you had a certain amount, and it got used up. The bravest man on earth could run out of it, if things went on too long, Daddy said, and it could take years to get the bucket filled up again.

And now Pat was using his already, and they had been out just about half an hour, and the whole task was still ahead. But nothing could be done about it now. Well, he could consider telling Pat he would put him off at Folke-stone, to get the bus back. John turned this idea over in his mind as they ploughed northwards.

The mist was lifting rapidly. The sun was warm, and John pulled off his duffle coat. There was still no sign of other little boats. The Dymchurch wall was left behind, they were sailing now along jagged rows of cliffs. They weren't really white, but grey and blue, with white streaks. It was funny, thought John, that the land looked much less solid when it ended in cliffs. The low line of the wall looked like a firm boundary drawn between the water and the land; but these great cliffs were the bones of the land, bared to the eye, with the waves fretting and eating at them for ever and ever. Surely the sea would win, would chew the land into endless sands.

"But I won't be here to see it, after all," he thought, and he reduced speed, for the piers of Folkestone har-bour were approaching. He saw a car climbing the road over the cliff, and was struck with astonishment that anyone was still doing anything so ordinary as driving a car, while he and Pat were here.

Pat put his head out of the cabin. "We got there, then?" he asked.

"This is Folkestone, Pat," said John. "I thought if you were still feeling rotten, I could put you down here, and you could get home on the bus."

"No go," said Pat, in nearly his usual voice. "I haven't got the fare. Unless you could lend it me?"

"Sorry, mate," said John laughing. "I've come out without a penny in my pocket. Rather far to walk, I'd say."

"Yea. I'd better stick it out."

At Folkestone there were things happening. Some small ships were coming and going; and there was a big steamer lying offshore, waiting for her turn at the quay. Her decks were crowded with men in khaki. A lifeboat had just left the harbour, and was making up the coast towards Dover. John opened up the throttle again, and gained on her. Then he kept a little way behind her, and simply followed. Behind him another speed boat, and a fishing boat came up, and a line of craft going in the same direction could be seen further out to sea.

"Come and take a turn at the wheel," John said to Pat. Pat's steering was a bit wild at first, but he was quite steady on his feet now. John showed him how to line up the prow with a point on the coast line, curving round ahead of them, and keep it in line. The engine controls were simple enough. Pat got the hang of it all very quickly.

"It's like steering a car, only it's slower to turn," he said. "Like driving a car through treacle."

"How do you know? You're too young to drive a car."

Pat made a wry face. "Rum sort of geezer you are, John. As grown-up as me grandad one minute, and green as a new-born babe the next, that's you."

A few minutes more, and Dover came in sight.

"Blimey!" said Pat, "It's like Liverpool Street in the rush hour!"

Spread out for a mile outside the harbour was a great cluster of shipping. There were half a dozen big steamers, several destroyers, many smaller naval vessels, and a great countless swarm of tiny boats, like flies round jamjars. John studied this scene through his binoculars. Many of the boats were coming in; he watched carefully the movement of boats putting out to sea. He knew that a route would have been cleared for them by mine-sweepers before any of this could have started, and he wanted to be on that route. When he sorted out the direction in which the departing vessels were moving, he took the wheel from Pat, who would have liked a longer turn, and steered in a wide seaward arc round the clustered ships. He had his cap pulled well down, but he didn't want to go too near any of the official-looking ships in case anyone decided they were too young, and tried to stop them.

The stream of ships which *Dolphin* joined was an extremely odd collection. Two pleasure steamers, the lifeboat they had followed from Folkestone, and a tug towing some twenty Thames barges were their immediate neighbours. Ahead of them stretched a line of blobs, all that the eye could make out of more ships and more still, all the way to the horizon. There didn't seem any reason to take a place in the line as though it were a queue, so John opened the throttle, and let *Dolphin* speed past the tug and her burden. They went faster than most of the other craft, and so they overtook and passed the strange procession one by one, and England shrank out of sight behind them.

Chapter Twelve

THE coast of France started as a thin line of mist on the horizon. It was mid-morning when it became clear in the circle of John's binoculars. The country behind the coastline was flat, for there were no hills to be seen, but there were a lot of rolling sand dunes and wide beaches, stretching for miles. Scanning this alien shore John saw a group of houses behind the beach; the sea-side end of a small town.

They were still following the route of many companion ships and boats. They had come much further north than John had expected, going round the Goodwin sands, and then striking southeast towards France. John supposed that the German guns at Calais had closed the more direct route. Now they were moving in southwards, and that great cloud of black smoke a few miles to the right must mask the town and port of Dunkirk.

The sun was shining. The whole scene looked like one of those great paintings of sea-battles, with modern ships instead of galleons. All around them, up and down the coast as far as they could see, there were ships of all sizes. Big naval ships painted silver-grey were standing offshore, and among them a motley collection of cargo and passenger ships. Beyond them was a stretch of patchy water, blue and indigo, and green in the warm light. And across these wide shallows hundreds of little ships were swarming. There were wrecks too; small boats capsized and drifting, and larger ones grounded and smashed. They sailed through a great patch of floating oil, which stuck to *Dolphin*'s paint. And there seemed to be a lot of oil washed up on the beaches; irregular dark shiny patches spreading over the sands to the water's edge. The beach was littered with abandoned lorries and tanks. It all looked very confused.

But it was clear enough what the small boats were doing; they were ferrying to and fro between the shore and the big destroyers and great ships which could not get further in.

They took *Dolphin* close under the bows of a great destroyer riding at anchor in the sea lanes, and moved towards the shore. Then they saw that the dark patches on the beaches were moving; flowing slowly like spilt water on a flat plate. It wasn't oil; it was great crowds of men. They stood in wide masses on the sands, and the sun struck a dull metallic glint off their steel helmets. Great groups of them moved slowly down towards the water's edge. Long lines of them snaked from between the dunes, and the head of some of the lines stretched out into the water. They had waded out shoulder deep, and they stood there, quietly, looking all one way—seawards.

John took *Dolphin* in towards one of these lines of men. They could hear a distant noise of guns—a low rumble and now and then a big bang, muffled by distance. But somewhere overhead there was also a droning sound. It got louder and nearer. Looking up, John saw a great swarm of black planes coming from the landward sky. On the beaches men were running for shelter among the dunes, or flinging themselves on their faces in the sand. The planes swooped down, diving low, and flying along the line of the beaches. John saw the black bombs falling in diagonal formation from the swiftly moving planes. A line of fountain-like upward spurts of sand ran along the beach, among the groups of helpless

96

men. From the heart of each jet of sand came a flash of fire, and clouds of thick black smoke. A man with his body stiffly spreadeagled was thrown high in the air, and shot backwards twenty yards from one of them. Then the noise of the explosions crashed round *Dolphin*, wiping all other sounds out entirely, and the beach they were heading for disappeared behind a thick blanket of smoke, which rolled across the water to meet them. A great blast of air smote *Dolphin*, and rocked her violently, and then they were wrapped in blinding, choking smoke.

They coughed and rubbed their eyes. Pat was saying something, but there was only a deafened ringing noise in John's ears. Helplessly he watched Pat's lips moving. The smoke rolled over them and away. They could see to the left now flashes of fire from the muzzles of skyward guns behind the long mole of Dunkirk harbour. A long mole extended seawards on the near side of the harbour, and large ships were tied up there. From the decks of these great ships avenging guns stammered angry retorts into the sky.

On the beaches men were getting to their feet again, and stumbling back into formation. From among them a number of pairs of men were tramping wearily up the beach towards the line of buildings, each pair with a limp body extended between them. The sun broke through the smoke in misty patches over them.

The planes did not go when they had dropped their bombs. They came back again and again, flying low over the beaches, and the shallows, machine-gunning the soldiers and the little boats. A hissing line of bullets spattered the water just in front of *Dolphin*'s prow.

John's hands were clenched on the wheel, but his arms were shaking violently from shoulder to wrist. He could hear his teeth chattering, and a hard lump had grown in his stomach, and was pressing against his ribs, so that he had to force himself to breathe. He stood at the wheel, shaking, and *Dolphin* moved steadily in towards the shore. A smoky haze blurred the whole scene. A choking, bitter smell of burning smarted in John's nostrils at every breath. Pat had gone white, and was crouched down against the bench. His pale eyes looked dark; the pupils were widened with fear. John fixed his eyes on a point on the beach ahead, and tried to steer for it, though he could scarcely make his trembling arms move his clenched fists. A lifeboat, full of soldiers, was just being pushed out into the waves ahead of him. He steered to come in beside it.

The planes were coming back again. The noise of their engines as they plunged low over the sands roared in his ears. He looked, and saw one of them coming straight towards *Dolphin*. He flung himself on the cockpit floor, and at the same moment Pat dropped down beside him, and the wave of noise and the sharp cracking of the plane's machine guns went over and past them. They were still alive. They got up.

Where the lifeboat had been there was a blazing wall of flame on the water. Someone was screaming. The flame floated towards them, and sank. John took the wheel, and brought *Dolphin* on course again. She chugged slowly through charred lumps of floating driftwood, until a gentle scrape on *Dolphin*'s keel told him she had grounded. The tide was low, and a stretch of shallow water still lay between them and the sand. John put the engine out of gear. The two boys stood and looked round. The water was full of floating bodies. They stained the froth on the waves with faintly visible red streaks. They rolled to and fro in the surf. Some of the soldiers waiting in line on the beach had run forward, and were dragging limp wounded figures from the water.

The hard lump in John's stomach suddenly lurched

up his throat. He staggered to the side, doubled up, and vomited into the water. As he hung there the body of a man with no face floated by, smelling of charred flesh. He was instantly doubled up again, retching on an empty stomach. Then Pat's hand was on his shoulder, pulling him up.

"Snap out of it, mate. Here's some poor blighters wanting a lift out of this." Pat's voice came from far away, sounding tight, and unduly loud.

A group of soldiers were wading out towards them, holding their guns over their heads. They came right up to *Dolphin*, and stood waiting, waist deep in the sea. Pat took their guns, and John told two of them to hang on to one side, to steady *Dolphin*, while others scrambled over the other side. The water poured from their clothes onto the cockpit floor. They took eight on board, and then John thought they were low enough in the water, and turned the others away. The men who were left pushed *Dolphin* off the sand, grunting under the strain, for she was weighed down now, and turned to scramble through the waves to the beach again.

An agonized expression crossed Pat's face as they went.

"We'll come back for you!" he called to their retreating backs.

"If you don't get sent to the bottom first!" said one of the soldiers beside him.

John was getting used to the different feel of *Dolphin* with her heavy load on board. She was sluggish, and slower to respond to the wheel. Still, when he gave her full power she roared away from the terrible beach towards the tall destroyer waiting off shore.

Over the side of the destroyer hung great swathes of coarse rope netting, draping her wall of riveted plates from stem to stern. Small boats bobbed alongside her all the way, and out of them swarms of soldiers scrambled up the netting, to be pulled over the rails to the decks.

John took *Dolphin* up alongside, nosing carefully between two drifters, from whose crowded decks hundreds of climbers were slowly and jerkily heaving themselves away. *Dolphin*'s eight men clambered out of her, making her rock and sway with their movements, and merged with the throng.

Gently John backed *Dolphin* away. When he was clear he gave the wheel to Pat, and looked back at the destroyer through his binoculars. Absurdly, he caught himself trying to find the men they had just put safely on board, but of course on the thickly crowded decks he could not find them. He picked out somewhere amidships a little board with the name WAKEFUL on it in brass letters. At her bows she carried her code number, painted in huge white letters. John regarded her with satisfaction. She was big, and strong, and armed with her own guns, and the men on board her were going safely home.

As they went back towards the beach, leaving a foaming wake behind them, the attack began again. But this time it was different. John felt oddly numb, almost light-headed. He saw the exposed position of his own body, sitting in *Dolphin*'s cockpit, as though he were outside himself, seeing the danger from a safe place a little way off. It wasn't really him being fired at; he was somebody else; somebody he didn't really care about much. Pat held the wheel quite steady, and John could hear him in the brief gaps between the deafening noise of exploding shells, cursing volubly in his everyday voice. John listened to the stream of foul language with admiration. He himself knew very few rude words.

The continued shattering noise, the confusion, and this strange feeling of being outside oneself, numbed, moving in a daze, blurred John's memories of the hours that followed, so that he could remember them only in patches, and could not have said clearly exactly what they did. They did what all the others were doing; they went in to the beach, picked up a load of men, and took them out to the *Wakeful*. They did it again and again, for hours on end, and John's memory would not sort one journey from another; they were all alike.

He remembered heaving wet bodies over the side into the cockpit. He remembered how they made *Dolphin* take eight men; two on each bunk, two on the cabin floor, two on the benches round the cockpit. Pat kept wanting to pack men in standing up, and so take more, but John was worried about the possibility of capsizing or foundering, if they loaded her too much; as it was she hadn't been built to take eight.

He remembered the roar of the engine, and the swoosh of water as they raced out to the destroyer. Then the grey towering wall of riveted steel, the swinging nets and ladders, the dipping and rocking of *Dolphin* as tired men dragged themselves clumsily out of her and up the side of their homeward-bound ship. And then they went back for more.

Sometimes they went in sunlight, sometimes in black smoke. There were hundreds of other boats bustling along, loaded with men, standing so thick on their decks that they couldn't move without pushing one of their number into the water. The buzzing planes overhead did their best to thin them out. John remembered seeing men falling from the decks of a drifter which was getting peppered with bullets. He felt a wave of anger against the German pilots who shot down such helpless victims. Then he realized that our own pilots would do the same, if the positions of the two armies were reversed. And it struck him suddenly that it was this sort of thing which Andrew had refused to do. For the first time a glimmer of understanding of Andrew's ideas entered his head. But he had no time to think about it. The next second a crackle, a smacking splintering noise of *Dolphin*'s timbers sent him scrambling forward. There was no bad damage done, but a line of holes disfigured the foredeck. Pat made an obscene gesture at the sky. He looked extremely cheerful and quite unafraid. *There is at least as much courage in his bucket,* John thought, *as in mine. More probably.*

Although it was for the sake of all those soldiers that they were there at all, John remembered least of all about the boatloads of men. They were all tired, and wet and cold. Tired most of all. Not the tiredness which makes one sleepy, but a terrible weariness of body and mind, which made them slow in all their movements, and glazed their eyes, and made their faces blank. Pat was very good at managing them. He called the men "Mate!" and the officers "gaffer!" and he shouted "One more inside!" and "Hold tight!" just like the conductor of a London bus. He raised grins on tired faces, and nobody seemed to mind doing what he told them.

Of course, some of the passengers caught John's attention, and so he remembered them later. One officer said to him, "I've got a boy about your age," and produced a soaking wet snapshot to show him. It was of a boy in scout's uniform. There was one group who came aboard every one still carrying pack and rifle, unlike most. In charge of them was a very quiet officer, and a very fierce sergeant, with a round baby face, who yelled at them as though he had them on parade. They waded into the water in a line as straight as a ruler, and they were much more cheerful than most. They even sang as *Dolphin* took them across to safety in the *Wakeful*. The song was about the round-faced sergeant. It went to the tune of "It's a long way to Tipperary." The words made even Pat raise his eyebrows.

Towards evening, in one of Pat's spells at the wheel John poured some of Crossman's soup into mugs for supper. They drank soup and ate biscuit without stopping; one hand was enough to steady *Dolphin*'s wheel. They had got used to noise, and the gunshot, and the blast from bombs and shells. They didn't jump any more, they just carried on. But the evening seemed long. They were very tired now. But at last dusk crept up upon them.

And with the dusk, slowly, so that they hardly noticed it at first, the fighting died down. No more planes came over, the guns on shore fired only sporadically, and there was a lull. They went back to the beach in the unaccustomed quiet, straining their eyes in the half-light. A small motor cruiser which had worked beside them all day was going in the same direction a little way off on the port side. Looking towards her John saw a dark round shadow bobbing in the water in front of her. The next instant she had struck it.

The explosion stunned John. He struggled to see and hear, to realize what had happened. A great wave had washed over *Dolphin*, and he was standing in a few inches of water.

"Pat!" he called. "Pat, where are you?"

"Here," said a voice at his feet. Pat had been knocked over by the blast. He scrambled up again, and they looked for the little cruiser. There was not the smallest trace of her. Pat was looking at John in alarm. And John realized that there was a nasty hot, wet feeling in his left arm. He looked down at it, and saw that he was pouring with blood. He felt weak and faint.

Pat did not panic. He got John lying on a bunk, and pulled his arm out of the sleeve of his sweater. He opened the first aid box Crossman had given them. There was a ragged piece of metal stuck in John's upper arm. It was bleeding profusely. Somehow Pat got the thing out. John was looking the other way, biting his lip. It didn't hurt as much as he feared; it was still numb, but the iodine Pat used to clean it up with hurt so much

103

he could hardly stop himself crying out. Pat put a lot of bandage round his arm, and then got the brandy bottle, and insisted that John drank some.

"I'll be all right now," said John, getting to his feet. "Thank goodness it was my left arm, and not my right." As he spoke they heard shouting, coming from just outside. *Dolphin* had been drifting, and had nearly run aground on the beach. And a mob of soldiers were scrambling out towards her, shouting. "A boat! A boat!"

John grabbed the wheel, and swung it hard round. The prow turned away from the beach, bringing her sideways on the shore. A stab of pain from his shoulder stopped John's hand halfway to the switch to put the engine on. A dozen hands grabbed *Dolphin*. She tilted down towards them. A rabble of hysterical men were all trying to board her at once.

"Let go!" cried John. "You'll capsize her!" Pat grabbed a saucepan from the galley, and laid about him like a fishwife, smashing at the knuckles of the raiders, banging them till they let go. Cries and curses rang through the growing darkness.

Suddenly a voice from the shore cried, "Let go that boat!" A man waded out towards them. He was only a private, but he still had his gun. One of the mob had succeeded in getting aboard. The newcomer looked up at him.

"You're an officer, aren't you? Where are your men?" There was no answer. Then, very slowly, the officer got over the side, and let himself down into the water. He waded away towards the beach.

"Right. One at a time now." The private got them aboard at gun point. "Had a rough time, this lot," he observed to Pat, as though talking about the weather. But now they were aboard they seemed just like the rest; tired, silent, wet, with that expression half-way between blankness and patience on their faces.

John put *Dolphin* full speed ahead, and made for *Wakeful* again.

"You all right?" asked Pat anxiously.

"Fine," said John. But his arm hurt, and he let Pat take the wheel. Pat managed it well, even the tricky manoeuvre edging up to the side of the destroyer.

"Don't take long to learn to drive these things," he observed.

John grinned. "Wait till you meet some real weather!" he said.

When they reached *Wakeful*, her officers were leaning over the rail. "Last few now," they were calling down. "We can't take any more. We'll be back tomorrow, God willing!"

Pat helped their passengers onto the ladders. Looking up to see them go, John saw stars pricking the wide black sky. His legs felt soft and bendy. He sat down. Under his instructions Pat took *Dolphin* out half a mile, to the sand-bar which bounded the sea-road along the shore. Here the water was shallow, and they let out the sea anchor among a group of drifters and tugs, whose crews were also taking a brief rest, under cover of the welcome night.

They drank some more of Crossman's soup, and ate plenty of the funny coarse biscuit with guava jam. It all tasted very odd, but it was filling. Then they lay down on the bunks to get some sleep. The bedding was soaking wet from having been sat on by all those wet soldiers, but John was too exhausted to care. He was asleep almost as soon as he lay down.

Chapter Thirteen

JOHN dreamed that they were surrounded by frantic men trying to climb on board; one of them had him by the arm, and was dragging at him, trying to pull himself up. The boat seemed already to be full of water; he felt wet and cold. Then he opened his eyes. Above him was the roof strut of *Dolphin*'s cabin. He felt himself floating gently. *Dolphin* was almost still, quietly riding on tranquil water, but the slight, smooth movements of her hull gave him the sensation of floating. The water he felt must be in the cabin. He woke abruptly, and sat up. She was sinking!

He looked at the dry floor boards of the cabin for several seconds before he realized that it was only the bedding in the bunk he lay in which was wet. The damp had soaked through his own clothes to his skin, and he was shivering in his clammy garb.

He got out of the bunk. But the sense of danger had not left him; hadn't there been boarders? No; the dragging at his arm was only the tightness of the bandage on the sore wound. The noise of the scrabbling, grasping hands was only a light scratching tapping noise on the side of the hull. Suddenly he remembered the mine which had blown up the motor boat yesterday. His heart was pounding and his tongue had gone dry. He went to look what it was.

A thin grey light filtered through the cabin door. Outside, it was light, but a white mist hung over the sea, shutting everything out of sight. None of the ships that had been anchored around them the night before was visible. The noise on the side of the boat was made by a drowned man, washing gently against her. He floated face upwards, and the water lapped into his staring eyes. John felt a surge of relief, but the glint in the man's eyes made him turn away shuddering. He fended him off with the boat hook.

Back in the cabin Pat was still sleeping soundly. John opened the flask of coffee Crossman had given them. What remained in it was cold and horrid. He slopped it out of the porthole, and put a kettle on the stove. There was a small locker in the galley, where food was kept when the family took *Dolphin* sailing. John found three old, battered tea-bags, and some lump sugar lying in it. He made tea in a big saucepan, refilled the flask, and poured two cups from the pan. He worked clumsily, using only one hand; his hurt arm was now very stiff. And the quietness quickly got on his nerves, so that he was glad when the tea was made, and he had an excuse to wake Pat.

"Did you hear that bang in the night?" Pat asked as they drank tea, and chewed more biscuit.

"What bang?"

"Cor, if you had heard it, you wouldn't need to ask. One helluva bang, there was. You must have been out like a light; it would have woken you otherwise."

"A big bomb, I suppose."

"Came from out at sea somewhere."

"Oh." John couldn't summon much interest in it.

"You reckon we ought to scarper off home?" asked Pat.

"No, not yet. Unless you've had enough, Pat. I wouldn't blame you. Don't be afraid to say."

"Not me. And there are a heck of a lot of soldiers still on that beach. I'd bet *they've* had enough. I was thinking of your arm, mate."

"I'm OK. But you'll have to manage the boat most of

107

the time. I don't think I can handle the wheel much. My arm's very stiff this morning."

"That's all right. I can steer your boat easy enough."

"If we have another calm day ..." thought John to himself.

There was still nothing but mist outside. They had to use the compass to work out which way to head for the beach, although when they looked up they could see a pale blue sky with some clouds in it. The mist was only a few yards thick; only a haze on the surface of the water.

"It's good cover, anyway," said Pat.

It muffled sound as well as sight. They were quite near in before they heard the gunfire rolling from the hinterland behind the beaches. But they had not heard it for many minutes before they knew that it was nearer than it had been yesterday; the rearguard had given a few miles. It proved impossible to work as they had done yesterday, because there were no big ships there to take on men. With Pat at the wheel *Dolphin* nosed up and down the coastline a mile or so both ways, but there was no doubt about it; there were no big ships about.

"They've all gone off home, and haven't got back yet," said Pat. "What do we do now, skipper?"

"We could hang around for a bit, and see if one turns up. I suppose it would be worth waiting till noon; but we have to start back early in the afternoon; we mustn't risk running out of petrol in mid-Channel."

Hanging around wasn't much fun. They couldn't see far in the wreathing sea-mist, and they decided to save petrol by switching the engine off, and just letting her drift gently. Pat smoked a lot of the cigarettes Crossman had given them. John just sat. It was very nasty, being so close to danger, and having nothing to do to take one's mind off it. But they didn't have to wait till noon; long before then a filthy battered coal-carrying tramp ship arrived in the sea lanes, and appearing miraculously out of the dissolving mist, a handful of little boats began to ply between her and the shore.

John turned on *Dolphin*'s engine, and Pat took her towards the beach at random. They were both immensely relieved to be able to get to work again. The mist had dissolved into hazy sunlight, and the noise of battle was growing.

They found a change in the beach. The men had built themselves a makeshift pier, by pushing a line of lorries out into the water, and making a footway of planks laid over them. Men were scrambling dryshod over this gangway, and getting into boats drawn up at the end of it. A lifeboat and a small trawler were loading up, tied to either side of the last lorry, which was so deep that the waves washed over its roof. *Dolphin* joined them. It was much easier getting men aboard from the makeshift jetty than it had been yesterday; but it was harder getting them onto the ship. The tramp ship had no nets, only ladders, up which men had to climb in single file, painfully slowly. Pat became nearly frantic with impatience while they waited for their turn under the ladder, and then waited for their men to climb out one by one.

"Steady on, Pat," said John to him at last. "We are doing as well as we can. Best not to fret about it."

"We could get another whole boatload out here in the time its taking us to get them onto that ruddy ladder!"

"We won't do any better if we get worked up about it."

"At last!" said Pat, swinging *Dolphin* away as soon as the last man got one foot on the first rung of the ladder.

"Watch it, mate!" said John protesting. "You nearly gave him a ducking."

"We're in a hurry!"

"Don't be a fool, Pat. We aren't in a hurry. We just take it steadily, and keep calm."

Pat flushed. "Oh, yea. It doesn't matter how many we leave on them flaming beaches. We just keep calm!"

"I don't know what makes you think it matters less to me than to you." Anger made John's voice stiff and cold.

"The way you went on about them. 'England needs soldiers' you said. 'Save our army so they can fight again.' Just push them around the ruddy country like they was toys on your map. I don't give a damn whether they can fight again; I just want to get them out of here! One of the poor blighters what has to get left behind might be my dad!"

John's anger disappeared at once. He waited a long time before answering. "Well, can you think of anything we can do to work faster?" he asked.

"No, blast it, I can't," said Pat. He grinned at John. His anger too had blown over.

Dolphin pulled up again at the jetty. But before anyone got on board an officer appeared, and hailed them. He was carrying despatches, and he wanted a fast boat to take him north, and land him on some beach there, quickly.

"We'll be moving into heavy fire. You're free to refuse," he said curtly.

"'Op in, codger," returned Pat disrespectfully.

"As fast as she'll go, please," said the officer, getting in.

"My turn at the wheel now, Pat," said John, slightly alarmed at the thought of Pat's inexperienced hand taking *Dolphin* at full speed. He found he could use his stiff arm if he really tried. *Dolphin* sprang away, cutting a path between two walls of foam. The officer was looking from one to another of them.

"In the name of heaven, how old are you?" he asked.

"Old enough to handle a boat, sir," said John.

"You'd better put me down at once, and get home," said the officer angrily. "This isn't a playground!"

"Thought you was in a hurry," said Pat. The officer looked at them again. Their faces were streaked with black from the smoke; the set of their mouths, had they but known it, showed the tiredness, and the strain.

"How long have you been here?" he asked in a changed tone of voice.

"Since yesterday morning, sir," said John. Overhead they heard the droning noise of oncoming planes.

"Don't look up; they won't be ours," said the officer with bitterness in his voice. "Not a single one of our ruddy air force to stop them murdering us." Then in his normal tone. "Nearly at La Panne now. Can you get close inshore and put me off?"

The beaches here were being heavily shelled from the the shore. It was the same bedlam of smoke and noise that yesterday had been. But the protecting numbness had worn off. John was very frightened again, and Pat too was jumpy. They took the officer in to shallow water. Just before he jumped over the side he said, "Enough's enough. You've done your bit, and more. Get home now. I hope you make it." Then he was gone, wading towards the terrible inferno on the beach.

"He's right," said John, looking at his watch. "We'll have to get back now, if we're to be sure our petrol will see us safely home."

"You mean just quit, now?"

"Well, we aren't going home empty. Take her back to that crummy jetty, and we'll pick up a load of men to take with us." John had had as much as he could take of managing the wheel; he gave it back to Pat. They went back to Bray, where the crazy little jetty of half submerged lorries was still crowded with men. The coal ship however had gone, and the horizon was empty.

On the end lorry someone was directing the line of men. They came up in order, and scrambled down into

Dolphin. Pat held the wheel steady, and John, with his good arm, took such packs and rifles as the men still had, and told them where to sit. A little way down the line there was some pushing and scuffling.

"Right. That's all now," said John.

"Another bus along in a minute!" called Pat. A faint grin appeared on some of the weary faces in the row. Then the pushing arrived at the top of the line. It was caused by two men carrying an officer on a stretcher.

"Can you take him?" they asked John.

"I'm sorry, no." said John firmly. "We're full up."

The stretcher bearers were tired. They looked around at the dark sea.

"He should be in hospital," one of them said. A great silence had fallen over the waiting line of men. Nobody moved, nobody spoke. The man directing operations looked down at the water, as though it were no affair of his.

Then suddenly the man on the stretcher groaned. He stiffened, and tossed his head.

"Right, bring him down," said Pat. "We'll fit him in somehow."

"I'm sorry, Pat, but we can't." said John.

"Oh, have a heart, mate! We can tie the stretcher on the cabin roof or something. But we can't just leave him to rot!"

"We can't take him. We can't possibly. *Dolphin*'s too far down in the water as it is. We can't risk making her any heavier."

"One can't make much difference," said Pat. His mouth was set in a stubborn line. "If it's a risk, let's take it. We taken plenty already."

"I'm sorry ... but no. We have eight men on board, and ourselves. We can't risk ten lives for one. It isn't fair to ask it."

"It's a risk we got to take. You ain't really saying you

112

can look at that poor devil and say we're going to leave him? Ain't you human?"

"*You're* a flaming idiot!" cried John in exasperation. "This boat won't take any more, and that's that!"

"We've carried him for three days," said a voice from the jetty. "The morphia has worn off. He needs a doctor."

"I don't see why we can't put him on top of the cabin," said Pat sullenly.

John struggled to master his rising anger. "Look, you've only been in a boat for a few hours, Pat, and it's been the calmest day for years. If a bit of a wind gets up we'll be shipping water, and in bad trouble. We are chancing a lot on the hope that there won't be a swell in the Channel as it is...."

"It would be all right, then, if I got out?" said one of the soldiers from behind him. John turned to look at him. He was a lanky young man, with a cut on one cheek. He looked tired, and the empty expression on his face was unchanged as he spoke. John nodded.

"Rightie-ho. I'm off then," said the soldier, scrambling up the side of the nearest lorry. Several hands were extended to help him up, and to pat him on the back when he got there. Nobody said anything.

The stretcher was lowered down towards them. The man on it screamed when it hit the deck with a jerk. With a little difficulty they made room for the stretcher in the cabin, on one of the bunks. Then at last Pat took *Dolphin* chugging away from the jetty, and roaring across the bay. John was full of admiration for the unknown soldier who had given up his place, full of concern for him. "*I hope another boat comes for him soon*" he thought.

But when they were speeding up the sea-lane to the north, well out to sea, out of range of the guns at La Panne, and the sun shone through the grey afternoon, a great surge of relief and joy lifted John's heart. They

113

had done it; and what was more, it was over. They would be home in a couple of hours; they were out of gunrange already. The thought of home, with real food, and safety, and hearing things on the wireless instead of living through them seemed like heaven on earth.

Chapter Fourteen

IF he could have taken any satisfaction from it, John would have had the pleasure of being right. When they got out to sea a little way, and in open water, they found a light rolling swell on the Channel. It was not really rough; but the *Dolphin* rose sluggishly under her heavy burden, and it was clear at once that she could not manage at full speed. John told Pat to slow her up quite a bit. It would take longer to get back home, but that was better than shipping too much water.

Just beyond the offshore shallows, where they turned westwards and for home, there was a great wreck. A large ship had been hit by a torpedo, and broken in two. She had gone down in shallow water, and her two halves stood with a stretch of water between them. The broken sections amidships stood on the bottom, so that both bow and stern stood out of the water, grey jutting shapes ringed with white foam. John raised his binoculars to look at her. And slowly through his tired brain there dawned the realisation that the number on the bows was that of the *Wakeful*.

It was more than tiredness which made his mind so slow. For the first long minute after he knew what he had seen he did not think about it at all. Instead he watched the flight of a gull, which wheeled and soared gracefully, uttering its insistent cry. A thing of unfeeling beauty. But then it came to rest, choosing a perch on the hull of the ruined ship, and led John's eye back to the painted number. It was the *Wakeful*. She had split in two, and gone down. She must have taken with her nearly all of those on board. A great gust of rage swept over John. All that work; the long day yesterday, the danger they had borne, the risks they had run, all for nothing. All so that those hundreds of soldiers could drown instead of being shot. His mind shuddered away from the image of men drowning; men he had seen and spoken to, drowning; drowning trapped in the under-water spaces of the sunk ship.

It must have been a U-boat. John thought of the men in the U-boat looking into their instruments, care-fully taking aim, hitting, sinking, killing. He hated them. He imagined being able to revenge himself, and with savage pleasure he thought of kicking them in the face, breaking arms, letting rip with a machine gun, watching pain and blood. Then his frantic train of thought stumbled and stopped. Andrew said, "You can only kill a man if you hate him first. And it is always wicked to hate." Well this was hate. Now he knew what it felt like he realized he had never hated before. The cool, carefully measured tone of Andrew's voice crossed his mind like a subtitle to a picture of himself, hitting a German face with the butt of a pistol. "However wicked someone is, when you hate him you make yourself as bad as he is, or worse." *I am wicked to feel like this*, thought John.

But the thought only made anger blaze up in him again. *"It's all very well for Andrew, sitting comfortably at home, talking holy like a ruddy saint. He doesn't have to see this. How the hell would he feel, if this hap-pened to him? I'd like to see him try his ruddy forgiv-ing!"* His fury had brought him to the verge of tears. He felt weak with rage. His head felt oddly light and hazy. His hurt arm throbbed. The wreck of the *Wakeful* was left far behind, out of sight. Pat hadn't noticed. There was nothing but quiet satisfaction on his face.

All the way home the sun shone warm and golden, and the sea sparkled. They went the long way, round the north side of the Goodwins, just as they had come. It was the sort of day on which swarms of pleasure boats would have come out for the joy of it.

But that really made the nightmare journey worse. *Dolphin* chugged steadily along at half-speed. The wounded officer groaned and tossed on his bunk. A smell of burning had stayed in John's lungs, so that he kept looking at the engine housing in alarm, expecting to see smoke. Three of the men were terribly sea-sick. They hung over the side, in constant misery. All of them were desperately tired. They didn't talk. It seemed more than they could manage. Even at half-speed there was some spray from *Dolphin*'s wash. They couldn't have got any wetter than they were, but it made them colder, and the pleasant afternoon breeze cut John like a knife.

And then the man who sat nearest to him began to mutter to himself, and then to whimper like a child. The man sitting on the other side of him put an arm round his shoulder, and said softly.

"All right, son. All over soon. You'll be home again and tucked up in bed before you can say Jack Robinson. Promise." The man looked bewildered, but he stopped raving.

"He's a bit knocked up, this one," said his companion to John.

"Is he wounded?" asked John, looking anxiously in his direction.

"Not wounded. Upset. Some people get like it, after they've had a bit much. Shell shock. That's what it is." The shell-shocked man was sitting staring at his own hands, which lay in an odd attitude, palm upwards in his lap.

"*A Crossman to be,*" thought John. Then his eye fell

on the compass, and he concentrated on correcting the course, shouting instructions to Pat.

Pat glanced at the wretched man still doubled up with sickness. He was convulsed, but he was bringing nothing up.

"When did you lot last eat, then?" asked Pat.

"Three days," said the comforter of the shell-shocked man. He seemed so much more in command of himself than the others that the boys instinctively turned to him.

"We've got a little," said Pat. "We'll dole it out." Suddenly everyone looked more alive. All eyes were fixed on Pat. "What's your name, then?" he asked the masterful soldier.

"Reg," came the reply.

"Well, Reg, you just give the skipper here a hand," said Pat.

"How odd," thought John, *"to hear a boy younger than myself talking like that to a man of forty or so. Still, we're all in this together."*

The second bottle of soup was brought out of the engine, and poured into mugs. They passed round from hand to hand, and back to Reg, who refilled them. The biscuit was all gone, but John handed out chocolate. Then they rinsed the mugs in sea-water, and poured out funny tasting tea.

It was amazing the difference it made. They were all warmed and cheered by a little food inside them. When John produced cigarettes, and handed them round they brightened up still more.

"What you make of this, Reg?" called someone. "Ruddy Florence Nightingales, disguised as schoolboys."

"Can't be as young as they look, though," said Reg, "or they'd never have been let come."

"You're dead right, mate," said Pat, grinning. "Nobody let us!"

"Blimey!" said Reg.

But the good effects of the food soon wore off. They had had enough only to take the edge off their hunger, and now the sun was getting low, and they got very cold. The wounded man was tossing and crying out. Made bold by his success in dealing with John's arm, Pat let John take the wheel, and went in to him, and turned back the filthy rug which covered him. He came out again at once, looking very grey and wide-eyed.

"The brandy's all I can think of," he said. He looked so upset that John relinquished the wheel, and went into the cabin himself. The officer lay on one bunk. On the floor, and on the other bunk the other men were huddled, sleeping. John opened the brandy bottle, and slid his arm under the officer's head, raising him a little. Then he tried to pour the golden liquid down him. The officer choked, turned his head violently, and let it run out of the corner of his mouth. John tried again. And again. A lot of it came up again. He struggled to control his own heaving stomach. The cabin reeked of brandy, and the blood and sweat of the wounded man. But at last he started to get drunk. As he got drunk he swallowed more easily, and at last he fell into a painless stupor, and John left him, and went gratefully out into the air.

And there ahead of them, briefly golden in a little patch of slanting sunlight, was the most welcome sight in the world. The shining coastline of England stretched before them.

"Look there!" said John. Everyone looked.

"Well, that's a sight for sore eyes," said Reg in a shaky voice. John raised his binoculars to survey the scene. They were approaching Dover. A formidable cluster of shipping crowded the sea outside the port. And suddenly, from overhead, came that well-known spine-chilling drone.

The ragged chorus of voices around him, which had been bravely raising a song, fell silent. A squadron of enemy fighters roared overhead, and dived to attack the clustered ships. The ack-ack guns stuttered their ineffective reply. The sun went behind a cloud.

"We're not going in through that," said John decidedly. He simply hadn't the courage to face any more of it. The shell-shocked man began to talk again, deliriously, sickeningly. "Take us home, Pat," said John. Pat swung the wheel, and headed *Dolphin* southwards, away from the other ships. No Nazi plane would bother to follow one tiny boat all alone, when there were much easier targets to choose from.

They might have hit a mine, taking an unmarked route. But they didn't. They came close inshore just south of Folkestone. They sailed down the coast, along the well-known line of the Dymchurch wall, and they brought *Dolphin* safely in to Crossman's little pier just as the last crimson smoulder of sunset died out of the long receding levels of the marsh.

Chapter Fifteen

PAT jumped from the prow, holding the painter. But he didn't know how to tie the knot for making fast, so he had to stand there pulling the rope till John joined him. They helped the men out of the cockpit, and then went down into the boat again, to bring up the stretcher. As soon as John lifted it he felt an unbelievable pain from the forgotten gash in his arm. It was so intense it wiped out all other things from his consciousness. He dropped the stretcher sharply back onto the bunk. The man on it woke and groaned. Pat got Reg to help him carry it.

With his good arm John handed up the two packs and three rifles which they still had between them, and then clambered up onto the pier. For a moment they all stood around awkwardly, and then they walked along the pier to the wall.

"Blimey. Where's the land then?" asked Reg, looking at the drop below sea-level, and the flat featureless dusk beyond. It looked indeed like the ghost of living sea behind them. "Where the hell are we?"

"Romney marsh. Lydd camp is a few miles to the south." said John.

"How do we get there?" asked Reg.

"You don't. You come home with me, and get fed and dry first," John replied, making up his mind on the spot. He saw Pat glance quickly at him with eyebrows raised, but his confidence in his mother's ability to cope with emergencies was much increased since he had taken her to call at the railway carriage. Anyway there wasn't anywhere else they could go. The men certainly couldn't walk to Lydd; it was as much as they could do to walk along the track to the town and home.

They stumbled and swayed, and the man on the stretcher got a rough ride, and groaned at every jerk. But it was all they could do to carry him at all. John had hoped Crossman would help, but his hut was dark and empty when they passed. And the half mile seemed to their leaden feet and weary shivering bodies to have grown into ten miles of horrible rough going. The shell-shocked man whimpered, and kept sitting down. Reg was getting tired of him, and got rougher every time he pulled him to his feet.

It was quite dark by the time they reached the cottage at last. They all stopped in the yard. John opened the kitchen door. His mother was sitting at the table. She started violently, and looked round. Her eyes met John's. She got up without taking her eyes off him. She had been crying, and there were shadows under her eyes. She looked ten years older. But a slow expression of comprehension was dawning through the amazement on her face. She still stood there while John said "Come in" and the dripping little group crowded through the door, shivering with suddenly increased violence at finding themselves at last in the warm.

Then she said, "Of course! The boat. I should have guessed." John was pierced with remorse for making her cry and worry. The room swayed slightly. His arm hurt, and he wanted desperately to put his head on his mother's shoulder, and be put to bed, and fussed over. She was looking at him still, with an expression half-way between reproach and pride. Then the man on the stretcher groaned.

At once she came to herself. She looked around the miserable collection of men who had invaded her kitchen. "Bring the hurt man over here, and put the stretcher across these chairs," she said briskly. She looked at the others again. Their sodden clothes stuck to their bodies. "The rest of you, strip," she said firmly. "John, you and Pat come upstairs and help me find dry clothes."

They came down with a bizarre assortment of garments. All the contents of John's father's wardrobe, and most of John's own; his mother's dressing gown, and a lot of blankets. The boys took these into the kitchen, and went to get into dry clothes themselves.

The kitchen looked fantastic when they got back. It was very warm because the boiler stood in the corner. And now it was steamy with the moisture from damp clothes, and men wrapped in ill-fitting clothes and blankets sat around on all the chairs and on the floor, looking like comic indian squaws.

"Right lot of charlies you look!" said Pat jovially.

Mrs Aston came back, looked at the wounded officer, and turned back the blanket over him, as Pat had done. Then she very gently replaced it. She got a bowl of warm water, and sat beside him, and washed his face. He stopped groaning and looked at her.

"Hey, John," said Pat in a low voice.

"Get on the phone, John, and get the people up at the house to send a doctor, quickly," said Mrs Aston. And she sat holding the man's hand gently in hers. John's head had started to buzz. It was a distant, high-pitched noise, coming from very far away somewhere inside his head. But he made the phone call all right. When he got back he found Reg and Pat starting to boil kettles, and rummage the cupboard for food, his mother directing them. The shell-shocked man was sitting with his head in his hands, muttering and sobbing to himself.

The doctor came almost at once. He brought two orderlies with him. He glanced round the odd company in the kitchen, but he asked no questions. He gave the officer an injection, and the two orderlies carried the stretcher away.

"Anyone else hurt?" he asked looking round the kitchen. Nobody answered, but the doctor's glance came to rest on the man with shell shock, who was still murmuring crazily to himself. "You'd better come with me too," he said. The man took no notice at all, but remained sitting.

"You! Get up," said the doctor harshly. The man stumbled to his feet, and stood looking blankly like a sleepwalker. The doctor took him by the elbow, and steered him out of the door. "Good night," he said, as they went.

"Now then," said Mrs Aston, "I expect you're all hungry." She started to bring things out of the larder and set pans on the stove.

"Hey, John," said Pat urgently. "John I want a word with you..."

And then they heard the front door closing. Steps in the hall. And a voice calling which set John's heart thumping like a bird in an indoor room:

"I've tried every hospital, and every police-station in Ashford, and there's no trace of them." The kitchen door opened, and there stood John's father.

He looked at John, and an expression of boundless relief flashed across his face, quickly followed by one of anger.

"Where the hell do you think you've been sir?" he cried. "What the hell do you mean by it?"

"They took *Dolphin* across to France, dear," said Mrs Aston. John's father didn't seem to take it in.

"Leave this to me, Mary. I asked you where the hell you've been?" he said furiously. His father's anger was too much for John. He stood dumbfounded, hoping miserably that he wasn't going to cry.

"He's been fetching us home, sir," said Reg, getting to

his feet, and clutching his blanket around him. "And we're all ruddy grateful."

Captain Aston seemed only just to have noticed that there were visitors in his kitchen. He looked round at the curiously bundled men in blank amazement. A gradual understanding dawned across his face too. "Well I'm blowed!" he said.

Mrs Aston brought a steaming dish to the table. "Get some plates from the dresser, dear," she said to Captain Aston. She had heated together the contents of lots of hidden tins to make a makeshift stew; she ladled it onto plates, and handed them round. It tasted wonderful. *"Who but my mother, my wonderful mother,"* thought John, *"could put corned beef and pineapple, and carrots and peas in one dish, and make it taste good?"*

There was a deep silence while everyone ate. It was too important to be held up by talking. Then John's father went and got a bottle of whisky, and poured out some for all the men, asking their names and chatting as he did so.

"John. . . ." said Pat.

"You're a rascal, John," said Captain Aston, pouring a drink for John too, and handing it to him as though it were the most natural thing in the world. "Here's your poor mother, worried sick, and me going round all the hospitals for twenty miles around, expecting to find you in one of them after some dreadful accident, and all the time you're in a nastier spot still; and then here you come in as cool as you please, and say you've brought some friends for supper!" He looked round the faces of John's friends. "Who'd have a son?" he asked happily.

John sipped his drink in a haze of happiness. Even the buzz in his head danced.

"I thought you were in New York, father," he said. The back door closed behind someone going out.

"That letter had taken weeks to come!" said Mrs

Aston. "The post is so disorganized now. And I was so pleased to get it that I didn't look at the postmark. The letter saying he would be here yesterday hasn't come yet, and it was posted days ago."

"How is *Dolphin* handling?" asked Captain Aston.

"Like a bird, Daddy. But I couldn't have done it without Pat." John looked around for Pat to introduce him to his father.

But Pat had gone.

"Oh," said John. "Where's Pat? I suppose he's gone across to tell his mother he's all right."

"Oh dear," said Mrs Aston, "Isn't he here? I should have told him not to go over. Poor Mrs Riley couldn't sleep for worry, and she needed rest, so the doctor gave her a sleeping pill. He mustn't wake her now. I'll go and fetch him back." She slipped out of the door.

"Wait till you meet Pat, Daddy," said John proudly. Captain Aston went to the phone to arrange for a lorry from Lydd Camp to come and take his guests down there for the night. And in a minute Mrs Aston came back, looking puzzled, and said to John, "He isn't there."

"Blast," said John. "I do so want him to meet Daddy." Where could Pat have gone? He had nowhere to go except the stable house. And then a thought came over John's mind like cold sea-water over his flesh. He remembered Pat trying to catch his attention. How many times? More than once. What had he wanted? Could he have wanted.... No, surely not ... surely he couldn't be fool enough...

"I'll go and find him, mother," he said, running for the door.

"Come back, John," cried his mother. He plunged into the darkness, ignoring her cries.

"John! Come back! You're worn out, and you haven't even got a coat on!" John broke into a run.

He made for Crossman's yard. He hadn't the breath to

call out after Pat; he needed it all for the effort of running. Time and again he stumbled and fell, and dragged himself to his feet again, with his head swimming. He didn't have to lift his feet to run; the ground dipped and lurched upwards for him. There was a bright moon, and there were aircraft overhead, although there had been no siren warning, for he could hear them droning and droning.

The door of Crossman's shack was open when he reached it, and a bright pool of light splashed lawlessly through it. Crossman lay asleep on his bed, and the place smelt of drink. John ran on, past Crossman's petrol shed. The door of this too was open, though it was usually securely locked. Now it swung, creaking on rusty hinges. John ran on; to the pier. He knew before he looked, but still his stomach tightened as though he had been hit below the ribs when he saw.

Dolphin had gone from her mooring. Only the cold sea dipped and rose beside the pier. But the moonlight showed clearly enough the two petrol cans and the funnel lying on the pier, beside the vacant mooring. A smell of newly spilt petrol reached him. The pier stretched from under his feet like a black finger pointing out into the silvered moonlit sea. The droning got very loud. And the finger of the pier, like the needle of a compass when a ship's course wavers, began to quiver, and move round. Everything spun round and round, and John put his hands over his ears to block out the intolerable droning noise, and felt himself falling through the middle of the spinning world.

Chapter Sixteen

HE woke up in his own room. There was the ship in a bottle, and the wicker chair, and the sunlight pouring through the window. There was a fire burning in the grate; even in winter he had never before had a fire in his room. The gas mask had gone from his bedside table, and instead there was a thermometer in a glass, and a box of medical dressings. John lay and thought about these things. Somehow they were very hard to think about.

After a little while he tried to sit up. He couldn't. He didn't seem to be able to push hard enough against the bed to raise himself from it. But he rolled over, and reached out for a pile of letters which lay on the near edge of the table. The first he opened was from a school-friend. It was about the first eleven, and their prospects for the summer. It took John a long time to realize what it was about. The second one was a stamp catalogue. John had long since given up collecting stamps, but the firm had not yet given up sending him catalogues.

He felt tired, and left the other two unopened. He leant back against his pillows, enjoying the warmth and comfort of his own fire, and his own bed, but he didn't go to sleep. After a while, putting enormous effort into moving at all, he picked up another letter. It was from Mr Macleod. What could he have to say? Then while he was fingering Macleod's letter, he saw that the last envelope was a telegram.

He opened it. It said,

CONGRATULATIONS STOP   WOULD HAVE
GONE WITH YOU STOP

ANDREW

John looked at this for a long time without understanding it. Then suddenly memory swept back, and he remembered where he had been. How had Andrew learned about it so quickly, he wondered. He looked at the postmark on the telegram. It said "9.30 p.m. 3rd. June, 1940." So today must be the fourth. But that would mean he had been asleep for three days! He struggled to get up. There was something terrible happening, and he had to do all he could to stop it; he knew, but he didn't at all remember what it was.

Then there were voices downstairs. Footsteps came up, and the bedroom door opened. His mother was showing in the doctor.

"Well, well, awake today, and quite calm, I see," said the doctor. "Splendid."

"Have I been ill, mother?" John asked. She looked overjoyed and tearful at the same time.

"You have been suffering from physical and mental exhaustion. Quite natural in the circumstances, nothing to worry about," said the doctor briskly. But John could see that his mother had been worrying, natural or not. "Let's see that arm," the doctor went on. "Ah yes, healing nicely. A nasty ragged cut, but not deep." He took John's pulse, and then he left, and John heard him talking to Mrs Aston on the way downstairs.

He heard the door shut, and then his mother called joyfully to someone.

"The delirium has gone, and he's awake and talking!" She ran up the stairs again, and came laughing to take John's hand. "Oh, dear Janjan," she said. "Thank God you're better!"

A voice from the door said in mock sternness, "Don't call my son by that baby name, Mary!"

"Daddy!" said John. "What's been happening?" At the back of his mind was a terrible dread that he couldn't find the reason for, and he thought it might be the old sick fear at the way the war was going.

His father paled slightly, and shot a glance at his mother. "What do you mean, son?" he said warily.

"Well, I've been ill for days, haven't I? I don't know what's been happening. Has there been a terrible defeat? What's happened to the army at Dunkirk?"

Oddly, Captain Aston's face lightened a little. He sat down on the end of the bed.

"Yes, there has been a terrible defeat. We've been beaten out of France, and we've lost all our equipment, and we're certainly in a tight spot. But," his voice rose triumphantly. "We didn't lose the army!"

"We didn't . . ." John was bewildered.

"Of course, there are always many killed and wounded in heavy fighting. But apart from those, we brought them all home. People brought out their boats from all over the place—like you, John—and the navy ran it so well that we brought home the whole army, and a lot of the French as well. A third of a million men!"

A great wave of relief swept over John. He thought of those beaches cleared of hopeful, defenceless men. Empty beaches, and everyone safe. He smiled at his father.

"That's quite something!" he said.

"That's enough talking too," said his mother firmly. "Go to sleep again now dear, and we'll bring you your supper later on, and bring the radio upstairs for you to hear what Mr Churchill has to say about it all tonight."

But the awful feeling that something terrible had happened hadn't left John. If only his head would clear! It was droning again now. He gave up, and went back to sleep.

130

He was still drowsy when his father came up, and put the blackout over the windows, and switched the light on. His mother came too, bringing a tray of supper, the sight of which made John realize that he was very hungry. He sat up eagerly to eat. Mrs Aston put the radio on the chest of drawers. She sat on the end of John's bed, and his father sat in the little chair, and lit his pipe. The well known smell of his father's tobacco filled the room.

John's head still felt swimmy. He didn't take in the first part of the Prime Minister's speech, though he gathered it was about the grim and difficult situation. But one couldn't hear Churchill for long without listening; the gruff rolling voice compelled attention.

"... We shall defend our Island, whatever the cost may be," he was saying. "We shall fight on the beaches, we shall fight on the landing grounds, we shall fight in the fields and in the streets, we shall fight in the hills; we shall never surrender; and even if, which I do not for a moment believe, this Island, or a large part of it, were subjugated and starving, then our empire beyond the seas, armed and guarded by the British fleet, would carry on the struggle, until, in God's good time, the New World, with all its power and might, steps forth to the rescue and liberation of the Old."

With some food in his stomach, and these brave words in his heart, John felt himself again. He thought clearly at last. And he remembered.

"Where is Pat?" he said.

His father looked at him evenly. "We don't know," he said quietly.

"But ... but he took *Dolphin* ... and she only carries petrol for two days..."

"He hasn't come back," said Captain Aston.

John felt himself trembling again. He lay under the bedcovers in his warm room, and shook from head to foot. "No," he said. "No!" His father got up, and put an arm round his mother's shoulder.

"It's my fault," said John.

"No, Janjan, don't start thinking that," said Mrs Aston. "You mustn't blame yourself. And anyway there are lots of things that might have happened. He might have landed in Essex instead of Kent, and it's taking him a long time to get home; or he might be captured, and we'll get a letter from a prisoner of war camp in a week or two, saying he's alive and well...." her voice trailed away.

John was staring ahead of him, unseeing. He tried to remember Pat's face, and found that he couldn't.

There was a knock on the door downstairs. Mrs Aston went down. When she came back she brought Mrs Riley, carrying a white woolly bundle.

"Hullo, love," she said to John. "Your mum told me you'd woke up all right, and I come to see you."

John could hardly bear to look at her. "It's my fault," he said. "It was my idea."

"Go on," she said, sitting down in the chair. "You never told him to go haring off there again by hisself, I'll be bound. That wasn't no idea of yours. You don't know him like I do. Always off on his own, doing something daft."

"Mrs Riley is right, you know, John," said Captain Aston. "Of course, we know how you feel. We're all very sorry. But you can't take the blame for another boy's action. It was very foolhardy, very rash indeed."

"It was very courageous," said Mrs Aston, in a quiet voice.

"Yes, yes, but far too risky. He can't have known what he was doing. It really takes two to handle *Dolphin*; and this boy knew nothing about boats. You know yourself how many difficulties one can run into at sea." It was not to his wife, but to his son, that Captain Aston was talking. "And then it's one thing to go once; but you had put in two days and a night already. He must have been worn out, in no fit state to go anywhere. How was he going to navigate? And on top of all this there was the danger of mines, and of enemy action. He must have been very foolhardy, irresponsible almost, to take such risks."

But John would not hear of it. "No, Daddy, no, you're wrong!" he said fiercely. "He wasn't like that. He was brave. It was brave of him to go back. You don't understand. You didn't see them there, all standing, waiting. You didn't see them getting blown up because nobody got them off in time. He knew it was dangerous; he couldn't bear to leave them, that's all ... that's why he went back. And if he'd asked me, I'd have gone back too!" And then John remembered that Pat *had* asked him ... he had tried to catch John's attention, and John had not answered because his father came in, and he had thought only of seeing him again.

A funny little wail came from the bundle in Mrs Riley's arms. She came and put it on the bed beside John.

"It was my fault. I should have gone with him. How can you bear to speak to me?" he asked her wildly.

"Your dad's right, son," she said. "It ain't your fault." Her voice was husky. "And you're right too. He had guts, our Pat. His dad's right proud of him. You knew his dad got home? He come on one of the big ships. And it don't do to run to meet bad news. Pat may turn up yet. Takes a lot to kill a Riley."

John looked at her tired face, and saw at once that she did not believe it. "Have a look at Edith Angela, then," she said. "She looks like him, a bit."

But she looked pink and horrible to John. He barely glanced at her. Mrs Riley picked her up again.

"I'll get back to me old man, then," she said. Mrs

Aston went out with her. John heard her saying, "Thank you, Lily. That was good of you," as their voices moved out of earshot down the stairs.

Desperately John wished his father would go too. He could feel the hot prickling at his eyes that meant he was about to cry. The thought of crying in front of his father appalled him. He still remembered how disgusted his father had been the first time he took John out in a boat, when John was very small, and he had cried till they got back to dry land. But now he felt weak, and try though he might, the room was blurring in his eyes. He lay back on the pillow, and turned his head away from his father, hoping to hide his face.

"Look, son," said Captain Aston, "Crossman gave me this. Said he found it lying on his window sill." He handed John a cigarette box. It had a bearded sailor on it, and a ship. On one corner was written in large round hand-writing, *Ask John Aston to hold onto this for me. P. Riley.*

John opened the box. Inside was Pat's watch.

There was no stopping tears now. But Captain Aston was not disgusted. He came and put a firm hand over John's.

"You know," he said gravely, "in a war there are always people who lose friends, or family. That's what war is like. But you have saved something too. Think of the men you saved."

But John didn't even hear him; his thoughts were drowned, he couldn't think of saved men now.